**The *Babylon 5* Library
from Del Rey Books**

Babylon 5: *In the Beginning*

Creating Babylon 5

Season by Season Guides

Signs and Portents

The Coming of Shadows

Point of No Return

No Surrender, No Retreat

Babylon 5 *Security Manual*

Season by Season

POINT OF
NO RETURN

Jane Killick

The Ballantine Publishing Group

New York

A Del Rey® Book
Published by The Ballantine Publishing Group

™ and copyright © 1997, 1998 by Warner Bros.

http://www.randomhouse.com/delrey/
http://www.thestation.com

Library of Congress Catalog Card Number: 98-92945
ISBN: 0-345-42449-2

Manufactured in the United States of America

First American Edition: June 1998

10 9 8 7 6 5 4 3 2 1

Contents

Acknowledgments

This book would not have been possible without all of the wonderful people who gave generously of their time and their comments to make this book as comprehensive as it is. I would like to thank them and all the behind-the-scenes people at *Babylon 5* who were so helpful when I was doing my research, especially Joanne Higgins.

On a personal note, thanks to Liz Holliday and Andy Lane for their nuggets of information and advice and to Chris O'Shea and Dominic May for access to their video collections, and a special thank-you to David Bassom.

Special Effects

*B*abylon 5 would be a much more enclosed show if it were not for its special effects. Computer animation has allowed it to explore space in a way previous shows could have only dreamed of. Spaceships, planets, gunfire, and large and intricate space battles are all created inside the computer in a more efficient, cost-effective, and flexible way than was possible with old technology. *Babylon 5* was the first television show to rely heavily on computer-generated effects. In fact, it was so revolutionary that, in the beginning, nobody believed it could be done.

The man who made the evolutionary leap into computer graphics was Ron Thornton. Ron started his film and television career in 1979, doing special effects the old-fashioned way. In those days, spaceships and similar effects were all created using miniatures, scale models that were physically constructed and then filmed with an ordinary camera. Ron worked in the BBC visual-effects department in the U.K. before emigrating to the United States. One of the American television shows he ended up working on was *Captain Power and the Soldiers of the Future*, the science fiction show that first brought together *Babylon 5*'s production trio of J. Michael Straczynski, Douglas Netter, and John Copeland. It was in 1988, during a *Captain Power* postproduction session in Los Angeles, that the producers asked Ron Thornton to meet with them to discuss a new idea they had for an adult science fiction series. They hoped he might be able to provide the special effects for them and asked him to pitch for the job. In those days, they were still thinking about using miniatures.

The project went quiet for a couple of years after that, and it was not until 1991–2 that things started to happen again. By this time, Ron Thornton had become interested in computer animation, often known as CGI (computer-generated imagery) or simply CG (computer graphics). The method was still very much at the experimental stage, but Ron convinced the producers it was the way forward for

Babylon 5. "At the time, I hadn't got a clue how we were going to do it!" Ron confesses. But he produced a few test images that were enough to convince the TV executives, and pretty soon he had secured a job working on the pilot.

Ron Thornton and his company, Foundation Imaging, then went on to produce all the computer effects for the first three seasons of *Babylon 5*. This was usually done on a show-by-show basis. The number of shots for each show were worked out from the script, then the shots were divided up among the animators, whose main players were Adam "Mojo" Lebowitz, John Teska, Paul Beigle-Bryant, and Ron himself.

Shots would be constructed within the computer using a specially designed program. A typical shot of a ship flying through space is built up of several layers—the background, the ship itself, its movement, the movement of the "camera," and the lighting. This is worked out by using a wire frame (which is, effectively, a drawn outline) that represents the ship on the animator's computer screen. The animator then works out the ship's movement by plotting a series of "key frames" that follow the progress of the ship. The light sources (for example, a nearby sun) are then defined as well as any "camera" moves, such as panning to follow the ship. Once the animator is happy with the sequence, the computer is left to "render" it, which basically means coloring in all the pixels on the screen. For a typical *Babylon 5* shot back in 1993–6 that would have taken twenty minutes per frame, which at twenty-four frames per second is an incredible eight hours per second of film.

One of the most time-consuming, creative, and, ultimately, fun parts of the process is constructing the space-ships in the first place. The principles of doing this are very similar to the old-fashioned method of constructing and painting a physical model, in that the ship has to work in three dimensions and be painted and textured to look as effective as possible. The practical realities of doing this in a computer, however, are somewhat different. "Unlike building a real model, you've got to know before you start exactly how you're going to paint it," explains Ron. "Each of the surfaces has to be given a name to allow you to separate it from the other surfaces. So you've got to have a top wing, bottom wing, or fuselage or whatever it might be. You're thinking about a lot of that stuff, but if you're building a model it doesn't really matter; you make the whole thing, you spray it with grey primer, and then you think to yourself, 'What color am I going to paint this bit?' Something like the *White Star* is a nightmare to think about how you paint it before you start it because it's made of very complex, intertwining shapes."

Once the surface of the ship is colored in, or "painted," a texture is applied to make it look like a real object and less like a perfect computer creation. "One of the things that we really wanted to do was make sure there was a real richness in terms of the textures. So we would map everything, even if we used generic texture maps. We created a bunch of texture maps so that when in doubt, we would put this map on it and it would work, just like a standard metal-panel dirtied-down look. A lot of times when it was a rush, that's all some of the objects would end up getting textured with."

Another important component in convincing an audience that it is looking at real images is the lens flare that *Babylon 5* uses extensively. Lens flare occurs in ordinary live-action filming or still photography when light reflects within the lens of a camera. It is the sort of thing that camera operators try to avoid because they consider it an unwelcome intrusion, reminding the audience that they are watching something that had been photographed. The computer animator, however, is trying to persuade the audience that that is exactly what they are watching, and this is where lens flare can work to their advantage. "When I originally started talking with Alan Hastings, who was the writer of the program we use, that was one of the very first things that I requested," says Ron Thornton. "It's so important to get any kind of cinematic graphic look to it. It has to be really realistic from that standpoint. In the pilot it was a bit overdone; we didn't have many varying options on them, you could either turn them on or turn them off. It's much better now; we've got massive amounts of control over it. The lens flares now are made up of a number of different elements. There's a central glow, there's an outer glow, there's an initial light ring, then there's the interlens reflections, which, as the light moves across the screen, go in the opposite direction. You can have those for standard spherical lenses or for wide-screen lenses; the lens flares actually get squashed when you're shooting wide screen because it's a factor of the lens. We've got all of those features there now, whereas in the pilot it was on or off."

Another element that Ron Thornton and the producers were determined to bring to *Babylon 5* was a depiction of realistic motion in space. He describes it as "the one thing that I wanted to do more than anything." It was, he insists, not just a matter of producing pretty shots; a lot of thought went into the physics of living and working in space. The evidence of that can be seen in the early, pre-Thornton designs by artist Peter Ledger, based on suggestions by Straczynski. The *Babylon 5* space station was based, in part, on principles that appeared in Gerard K. O'Neill's influential 1977 science book on space colonies, *The High Frontier*. This aspect of *Babylon 5* earned the show an award from the Space Frontier Foundation.

It is also a philosophy that is reflected in the space battles. "A lot of it was trying to come up with a lot of techniques they would use in combat," says Ron. "Like the whole concept of flip and fire—flying alone, then turning around and firing backward. If you were in that tactical situation, being able to maneuver like that is going to be the only way to get away. If there's someone on your tail, you can't turn because there's no air. The only way you can do it is ballistically, so you'd have to alter the altitude of ship and blast. The whole concept of doing a turn like an airplane in space is totally impossible. So it was coming up with techniques that these pilots might use in that sort of environment, and that's what's interesting. The script for "Signs and Portents" had one really nice maneuver where Garibaldi had this particular ship on his tail. It's a three shot, so you have Garibaldi's starfury flying toward you and you see the ship on the tail, then the lower boosters on Garibaldi's ship push him out of frame and you get another shot where he's coming around and he fires. He ends up just coming up and pointing straight down at the guy and firing at him. It looked really great; the sequence worked really well."

There is, however, a certain amount of dramatic license with *Babylon 5*. Whatever else the effects might attempt to do, they have to make a dramatic impact. One of the ways that is achieved is by using color. "We wanted to make *Babylon 5* colorful," says Ron. "We wanted to use color to brighten it up. There had just been so many movies with grey spaceship after grey spaceship, and of course, I get my inspiration from things like *Thunderbirds* and *Captain Scarlet*, when there was loads of color."

One of the most work-intensive parts of the animation process is designing and building the spaceships used on the show. Joe Straczynski and other members of production obviously have their input, but a lot of the ideas come from the animators. One of the first ships to be created was the Vorlon ship, which had to look like it was based on organic technology. Science fiction cinema had been highly influenced by H. R. Giger, who had worked on the film *Alien*, but Ron Thornton wanted to explore a different avenue. "I wanted something that was a little bit different to the Gigeresque. When anybody would think of organic technology, they would think of Giger, the slimy, bony, evil, wicked-looking stuff. But a butterfly's organic, too, so why not have something a little bit more colorful?"

That was his basic thought, but it took a trip to San Francisco and a meeting with the people who produced his computer-animation software to inspire him to come up with the final design. "[My wife] Karen and I were driving back down to L.A. after this, and there's this little town called Gilroy, which is up in northern California, which is the garlic capital of the world. It just smells like spaghetti sauce when you go through it; it's great, just huge pots of garlic. It was on the way down the 5 [freeway], and I'm thinking 'garlic.' So I started sketching out in the hotel room the rough idea for the ship, and the head of it is basically a head of garlic, cloves of garlic. It's a cross between garlic, squid—it's a decent Italian meal when you look at it—you've got some calamari and you've got your garlic."

Another major ship design, perhaps the most significant in the whole *Babylon 5* universe, was for the Shadow ships. These vessels also needed to look somewhat organic and derived their surface texture from a scan of the nose of Ron's dog, Digby. "We knew we had to come up with something that looked pretty evil, and it had to be reasonably organic. Again, it was just an accidental thing. Karen, my wife, and I had been watching a Discovery Channel special on black widow spiders. They were doing all sorts of things like electrocuting them and making them bite into pieces of pork so it looked like it was on someone's arm; it was just so creepy. So that was pretty much where it came from. We wanted to get something that had that same kind of creepiness. I don't know if you've seen one in real life; they are so black they look like a little hole in space, spider shaped. Of course, black spaceships in space are a big problem. So we had to find ways to make it look interesting but at the same time predominantly a silhouette. Most of the time, you'd get a silhouette of this spidery-looking thing, but you also had a little bit of a feel that it was going to grab you."

The team at Foundation Imaging did most of the designing of ships like these, but on rare occasions, some illustrators were brought in to sketch out some ideas. This was particularly so in the beginning when some of the key elements, such as the Starfuries, were designed. "A very good friend of mine, Steve Burg, he and I codesigned the Starfury, the original one," says Ron. "There was another illustrator who came up with the original look for the Minbari cruiser. We sat and discussed it, that the idea was for it to be something between a butterfly and an angelfish and to have a lot of verticality to it. So we started working through ideas, and the thing he came up with didn't look like the ship turned out, but it gave me enough in terms of inspiration. It's like, 'Ah, I see something,' and then it would work. We've done that from time to time, have them come in and get rid of block. You get a bit of block, you get someone to come in and design something just whacky, and that starts to get you going again."

Foundation Imaging produced so many CGI shots for *Babylon 5* that they estimate the whole lot would make a feature film if they were edited together. There are so many highlights that it is impossible to focus on them all. But one sequence in "Messages from Earth," of the *White Star* returning to our own solar system, sticks in the memory for the beautiful rendition of the planet Jupiter. This was not animated from photographs of the actual planet but from an artist's impression. "A very wonderful artist friend of mine, Don Davis, does a lot of illustrations for people like Carl Sagan and stuff like that, and he had painted this image map of Jupiter. We paid him to have a license to use it. He'd done a proper cylindrical texture map of Jupiter by hand in water-colors. This piece of art is just so gorgeous, and we used that on the planet."

This explains somewhat why the people who worked on computer graphics for *Babylon 5* during Foundation Imaging's three-year tenure were not necessarily computer people. "I think they make the worst effects people." says Ron. "It's just because of the fact that you could teach someone who had ten or twelve years of art, effects, or filmmaking experience how to use a computer in a few weeks. But you can't teach somebody who is really good with a computer how to be an artist in a few weeks. You just can't. They can duplicate stuff that has already been done. Somebody could get the model of Babylon 5 and move it around. But to innovate? I think I was only just qualified to do this when we started, and now I don't think I'm qualified at all! It's one of those things, that the more you start to learn, the more you realize you don't know. I think that's what keeps it going. It's a massive arena in which to play out any artistic ideas you have; you can do just about anything."

It is one of the things that has made CGI so fulfilling for Ron Thornton and his team. Each animator on *Babylon 5* would be given a shot to work on from start to finish. There was no attempt to divide shots up so that one person would build the background, another would build the ship, and so forth. That way people got enthused about the work and felt a sense of achievement when they completed the job. *Babylon 5* also gave them a lot of freedom. There was minimal interference from the producers. They got a chance to let their creative juices flow, and that, says Ron, was the nicest thing about it. "It was extremely nice. I think it shows in the work. We've done some of the most innovative CG stuff that's ever been done for TV. And it's not for any other reason than that we really wanted to make it look great, we really wanted to make it look as good as possible. There are not enough people like that in the business nowadays, I'm afraid. And after a while it starts to get you down. There are very few people who are in it to do nice work—there are just too many people who are in it just for the money. If I wanted to do something for the money, I'd be a stockbroker or a lawyer or something; I wouldn't do this. I do this because I like it. It was a lot of fun. I still love the show. I still think it is so cool. It's not one of those things that happens very often. You don't often get the chance to do that, and when you do, how can you repeat it? How can you do that again? Something like that can only be different once."

In the fourth season, responsibility for producing the CGI effects for *Babylon 5* moved to Netter Digital, bringing the process under the same roof as the rest of postproduction and under the watchful eye of producer George Johnsen. "Realistically speaking, things have not changed much," he says. "Ron was a very large contributor to what the show looked like and helped realize a lot of the things that Joe came up with as far as ideas. He brought a lot of stuff to the party. We've continued to do that ... We've found that bringing the stuff in-house is a huge advantage to us in that we have direct communication now between animators and creators, and that's been a very interesting situation that hasn't happened before. So the difference is that we're bringing more to the party, not less."

There was much more reference to executive producer and writer Joe Straczynski and producer John Copeland in creating the CGI effects for Season Four, especially at the beginning, when people were getting used to the change in personnel. Certain computer-generated objects, such as the spaceships, could be taken from the library of shots built up over three years, but new things needed to be created. And for that, things proceeded very much as they did in the Foundation Imaging days.

"We'll just start off by drawing something," says George. "Like the Vorlon Planet Killer started off as a regular pencil-on-paper drawing, then the guys actually built a model of it in the computer and surfaced it with a Vorlon texture from the texture library. Then they added all the little bits and pieces that go on the outside—the fins, the weapons, the communications devices, all of that stuff. It then becomes a Vorlon ship, which we put into the ship library where we can pull it out and use it again if we need it. If you look at that particular object, there are lots of motion pieces in it. With Vorlon technology being organically based, lots of things move, lots of things change shape that you wouldn't really imagine to be changing shape. All of that has to be programmed in as some sort of motion path that actually allows the ship to move through space in a biological manner rather than being propelled by engines, as with EarthForce technology, or by using a crystal-based technology, like the Minbari. So we have all of those things that we have to take into consideration when a new shot is formed. Additionally, there are other things that have to happen; like if we're doing an establisher of Babylon 5 and we want to have ships parked around Babylon 5, we have to plot the whole motion path of where the ships are going to be, how they would be floating. Are they under power? Are they parked? All of that kind of stuff has to be established, then they have to follow the correct motion path so they don't run into each other, which could be an embarrassing situation!"

Another aspect of CGI is the compositing of live action with computer graphics. This has become a more prevalent technique in *Babylon 5* as the series has progressed. In the beginning, obvious shots that had to be a combination of live action and CGI were things like a pilot sitting in his Starfury passing by a starscape outside. This would be achieved in the traditional manner by filming the actor in the Starfury cockpit against a blue screen, using a locked-off camera that does not move. Then the starscape would be generated in the computer, and finally, the computer would be told to replace everything that is blue in the scene with the starscape. Since then the show has become more ambitious, combining more complex live-action shots with computer-generated material, especially in the field of virtual sets. It has even, on occasion, allowed directors to move the camera as they would in a normal live-action sequence.

"We plan the shot with the shooting crew," explains George Johnsen. "We come up with an approach that works, either move the camera, lock the camera, use a blue screen, use an edge matt that we actually cut out and place other things in. Then the thing gets shot. There's a supervisor from the visual-effects department onstage with the shooting crew, working with them to set up the shot so we actually get what we need in-camera. From that point, the film gets transferred to digital video. Once it's digitized and we have the material in digital form, then we start working on both the compositing side and the special-effects side. If we want to put Ivanova and Sheridan in the Observation Dome and do a big pullout, that element will start by itself. It will be a computer-generated window frame that goes around and on top of it, then we will place both of those things into the space station and move our 'digital camera,' if you will, away from the space station in whatever motion path we want and actually follow that away so you can still see the activity in the window."

A lot of the scenes combining live action and computer images rely on the talents of matte artist Eric Chauvin. When the characters appear in a setting such as the Zen Garden, only a tiny part, in the middle of the image, will be real actors and a real set; the rest of it will have been painted by Eric on his computer. "It gives the show much more scope than they can achieve with their limited stage space and fairly modest budget," he says. "There was a shot I designed which was a garden behind the Centauri palace. They made up a set which represents part of the garden and

had the camera fairly high up in the air so that the set elements are at the bottom of the frame, and everything else,
the painting element, I created. The way I work is to build
computer models and render them out, and then digitally
paint on top of that. If it's done correctly, it looks like these
people are in an exterior garden in an exotic locale."

Usually, in a shot like the Centauri palace garden, the camera will be locked off, but as technology and Eric's expertise
have improved, some of the matte shots have become more
ambitious. Moving the camera in one of these shots creates
complications because the edges of the frame, the amount
of space an object takes up on the screen, and the perspective will all change. But it is one of the things that can add
realism to a scene. "That's really what separates the good
image from the bad," says Eric. "You have to create something that is absolutely real. Unlike someone who's, say,
flying a ship around, where a viewer's going to know it's
an effects shot—you can't go out and film a spaceship—
my particular effects shots, you've got to make sure that
nobody can see they're effects shots. You have to be able to
believe it's real if you don't want them to go, 'Oh gee, that's
really fake.' Working on this show, because of the nature
of the imagery, it's easier to make things real. I've worked
on *The Young Indiana Jones Chronicles* [a historical action
drama], and that's something that has a lot of period buildings, a lot of exterior locales, but *Babylon 5* has a lot of fairly
simple geometric shapes."

Some shots require a lot more attention than others, and
that is where rotoscoping comes in. With this technique,
rather than producing key frames and allowing the computer
to fill in the blanks, the animator will separately animate
each individual frame of a sequence. An example of this from
the third season is when Delenn breaks the Grey Council
staff in "Severed Dreams." The energy that crackles through
the staff was so unique, it had to be animated one frame at a
time. This is also how the gunfire came to be produced in
season four.

"I'm proud of the gunfire," says rotoscope animator and
compositor Brian E. Battles. "It used to be done a different

way, and I worked on a lot of different looks for it until the producers liked it. First, I figure out when the shots are fired and who they're firing at—which can be a problem because sometimes extras have their guns up when they should be down—and I try to figure out the timing of the shooting. Hopefully they have a hand movement from which I can tell where they're shooting and when they're shooting. Then, frame by frame, I try to figure out how long it would take a piece of plasma to fly across this distance, and I put each piece in. After I'm happy with the timing, I put in the warp, that kind of warp effect, so it looks like it's really hot."

But ask the special-effects team what they like doing best, and George Johnsen's unequivocal reply is, "blowing stuff up. We use layer upon layer of effects stuff," he says. "We'll start with a back plate, which is what comes out of the camera. In front of the back plate will be a computer-generated something, and then we'll layer another live-action piece across the top of that. Then we'll put in an explosion over here, which is actually four or five explosions combined together."

But it is not practical or desirable to do everything in the computer. "Blowing stuff up" will often involve physical explosions on the *Babylon 5* soundstage, with sparks and debris falling over the characters. This aspect is the respon-sibility of Ultimate Effects, who use traditional film-industry pyrotechnics that look impressive but are unlikely to actually injure anyone. "We pretty much stick to propane gas be-cause it burns off fast," says special-effects coordinator Beverley Chargigan. "At the same time that we do propane, we do a debris mortar, which is a large air mortar that pushes out cork and particle board and light stuff that looks like pieces of the ship flying through the air."

For a large scene, like a battle sequence in which explo-sions fire off all over the bridge of the *White Star*, Beverley's team will spend a day and a half prepping the set—that is, laying down wires and mortars that will later throw out ignited gas and debris. Only on the day of the filming will they lay the actual charges and fill the mortars with propane.

These are all controlled off-camera by the pyrotechnician, who will fire them off on a cue from the director, actor, or, sometimes, stunt artist. All of this has to be prearranged during an all-important safety meeting.

"Before a special-effects scene is to take place, everybody involved—director, camera operators, the lighting guys that are going to be on set—have a meeting," says Beverley. "Only people who are absolutely necessary are allowed on set when we do special effects. We make sure everybody knows where they have to be, what's a safe area to be away from, and then they also discuss cues on how it's going to be set off."

Apart from the safety factor, it is important that things go right the first time because it can easily take two hours to re-rig the explosions on a set. *Babylon 5* rarely does two takes on a scene like this.

Fire can also add an explosive impact to a scene. *Babylon 5* tends to use fire sparingly, but it has been used to effect in several places, perhaps most notably in the bombing of the customs area in "Convictions." "We use what we call a fire-bar, which is a long tube. It can be any size that we want it to be; so if we want a really small fire, we can use a one-foot bar, but if we want a very large area, we could use a four-foot or a five-foot firebar. We hook this up to propane so that it's controllable. We can turn it up for the actual shots where they're filming so it looks like the fire's really raging, and when they call 'cut,' we can shut it down to a little pilot light, or we can shut it off and then just light it again. There was actually never any fire on the set itself; it is all done with the firebars and the camera angles."

Ultimate Effects' other responsibilities are manifold. They include operating the doors—which work on a pulley-and-winch system with a couple of guys on the end of a rope—and smoke effects. In the first two seasons, smoke was used all the time on *Babylon 5*, creating an atmospheric haze in many scenes. That lessened in the following years where smoke machines tended to be used only for crowd scenes in somewhere like the Zocalo or in scenes involving explosions.

In addition to smoke, liquid nitrogen has often been used to suggest an alien atmosphere, such as in scenes in Kosh's quarters, n'grath's lair, and the isolab.

Ultimate Effects also assists with the computer-generated gunfire effects by rigging up a physical explosion on the actor or stunt artist being shot. These effects are often referred to as "bullet hits" because of their extensive use in contemporary film and television productions that feature projectile weapons like pistols and rifles. "On a normal bullet hit, we would just use a squib that would push a blood bag, so you would get your hole and blood," says Beverley Chargigan. "On *Babylon*, they don't want to see any blood, so what we do is take one of our small sparks and rig it into a little tube so it is directional—it goes straight out. That's what we would actually rig on the wardrobe; we would cut a tiny hole in the wardrobe so that the sparks come out."

The other significant area of special effects that helps create the illusion of *Babylon 5*'s futuristic alien environment is the makeup effects produced by John Vulich and his team at Optic Nerve. Aliens like the Minbari or the Narn depend on prosthetic makeup, which is basically a textured and painted piece of foam latex worn by the actor.

"It's like three components that you whisk up," explains John Vulich. "It comes out a lot like meringue or shaving cream. Then you add this gelling agent into it; you put it into injection guns and squirt it into a mold. You have to get it in the molds before it solidifies or you won't get all the fine edges. Then it has to be cooked for four or five hours. It's like soap bubbles in a bathtub; it will start to collapse after a while, so it's a very tricky part of the operation. It's more like cooking a cake."

Once the "cake" has come out of the oven, it is trimmed and often prepainted before being put on the actor. "It depends on what the characters are," says John. "The Narns are all prepainted. On a lot of the Narns we use a template, particularly on G'Kar because we want it to match all the time, although you still have to go over it by hand. The Minbari's blue spot and flesh colors are prepainted. Some of the other races aren't prepainted. If they're just a face or forehead, it's not really worth it; you just do it on the actor. Like Peter's [Jurasik, Londo] makeup. They paint the red onto it as an underbase first, but they don't really do that until they get it on his head."

Applying the prosthetic piece to the actor is the final crucial stage in convincing the audience that they are looking at an alien. The time it takes to achieve this effect can often be deceptive. For example, Mira Furlan spends longer in the makeup chair being transformed into Delenn than Andreas Katsulas does to be transformed into G'Kar, even though he looks more alien than she does. "Her makeup takes almost twice as long as G'Kar's makeup. Andreas's makeup is an hour and a half, and the reason for that is it's really more of a mask. There's a little bit of blending around the eyes and mouth, but it's all mostly prepainted and there's just a little air brushing to tie the two together. Whereas her makeup is very fine, very sheer, especially in the fourth season it's almost paper thin. This forehead we use on her is very delicate. There's no wrinkles; there's no big black spots to hide any of the imperfections; it has to be as clean as we can get it. Then she has a hairstyle and a beauty makeup, so she has all these subtle things that don't look as complicated, but her makeup is two-and-a-half hours long."

Races like the Narn and the Minbari were all established in the pilot before Optic Nerve was brought on board, but many of the other aliens were designed by John Vulich and his team. Ideas for new aliens like Lorien, who first appears in season four, come from an initial reaction on reading the script, which is translated into a series of sketches that are then discussed with producers J. Michael Straczynski and John Copeland. "On some of the characters we have done, like the Markabs, we've done little eighth-scale designs, but usually we'll pin it down in a drawing. Then we'll do some sculptures of that and show them photographs, or sometimes we'll have them come by. Some characters they're very particular about, like Lorien. He was going to be seen in six or seven episodes, and they definitely had something particular in mind for him. Sometimes we'll have a test day when we try the makeup on and show it to them, usually with a costume fitting. Sometimes if the schedule doesn't permit, we'll do it the actual day we photograph them, but we'll allow an extra couple of hours to his actual makeup time so, if there are any changes to be made, there is time to do that."

The costume is, of course, an important part of any character, and John has to work alongside costume designer Ann Bruice-Aling when designing *Babylon* 5's aliens. "Ann and I always seem to be on the same wavelength with colors, sometimes without communicating early on," he says. "We'll meet together at one point and have a lot of the same ideas. I guess we both kind of approach things in the same way; I think we both try and approach colors emotionally. You try and think of a color being a symbolic aspect of the character rather than just being a pretty color. Again, that comes from the script and just trying to do something that fits in. Like with that episode "Infection," there was a mutated guy with a gun arm [the Ikaaran killing machine], and we tried to get his head almost like a Nazi kind of helmet so it kind of echoed that feel in a way that was not pretty obvious. I didn't want people to say, 'Oh, here's a Nazi suit,' but I wanted to have some subtle nuances that emotionally gave that idea. I think she does the same kind of thing. We endlessly find ourselves meeting somewhere and having the same ideas without even talking about it, which is kind of uncanny sometimes."

However, there are limitations to what can be achieved using prosthetics on a human actor. A person's face has distinctive features that are hard to disguise—eyes, nose, and mouth—and retaining these features is important in allowing the actor to put over a good performance. The dramatic potential of a creature like the Gaim (also known as the "hose noses" by the production team) is far less than that of a Minbari because it is harder for a human audience to relate to a character that has no facial expression. John Vulich's compromise on converting a human face into something more alien is to hide the nose. "That's the first thing I always try to do," he says. "A lot of people use this as a criticism, but for me it is the first thing I try to do. I just think that's the instant giveaway that someone is inside it. I don't mind the eyes and I don't mind the mouth, but the nose to me is just a real giveaway."

One way of solving the limitations of the human face is to use animatronics. Kosh, or at least his encounter suit, is effectively a puppet with remote-controlled servos that operate the eye lens and various fins on the suit, as well as the panel light that is operated by the person inside. The Pak'ma'ra is also a more radical design and is a mechanical puppet head with wiggling tentacles and blinking eyes.

All these elements combine to create the illusion that *Babylon 5* is a space station inhabited by a quarter of a million Humans and aliens. This is the setting that provides the basis for the story, and it is the story and the characters that are the most important elements. It would be possible to tell the story without such an impressive array of special effects, but it would not have quite the scope that it does. Special effects, particularly in the field of computer graphics, have allowed the characters to journey to places and to do things that would have otherwise been impossible for a television series. *Babylon 5* has been a pioneer in this sense and, since its inception back in 1993, has inspired other television shows to follow its lead.

Babylon 5's *Third Season*

Babylon 5, as the opening narration explains, was our last, best hope for peace, but it failed. Now it is our last, best hope for victory. 2260 is the year of the Shadow War, a year of building an alliance of forces to fight against the inevitable darkness that is to come. After two years of setting things up, *Babylon 5*'s third season really starts paying off, bringing together story threads that were once separate and tying them in to the Shadow War.

Babylon 5's first out-and-out confrontation with Shadow forces does not come until "Shadow Dancing," the penultimate episode of the season. This demonstrates how much the season is devoted to gearing up for that first fight, building alliances, achieving small victories, and learning about the enemy. It begins in the first episode, "Matters of Honor," where Delenn presents Sheridan with the *White Star*, a powerful warship based on Minbari and Vorlon technology. This is a departure for the third season, giving Sheridan and the others a means to leave the space station. It also gives the stories more scope, with an opportunity to venture into other parts of the galaxy. In this first episode, the *White Star* takes its first stand against a Shadow vessel and wins by destroying it in a collapsing jumpgate. This sets up the nature of the conflict that is to come, a David-and-Goliath struggle against a powerful enemy that can be defeated only through tactical thinking.

The episodes that follow rarely allow the audience to forget what everything is leading to, with continual references to the Shadow threat. Sometimes it is a relatively minor part of the episode, like Marcus being told Shadows are gathering on the border of Centauri space in "Exogenesis," sometimes it is the main thread, such as the search for First Ones in "Voices of Authority." If it were just a slow buildup with a promise of action that is fulfilled only after twenty episodes, the audience would be justified in feeling frustrated. But that is not what *Babylon 5* is about, as the creative force behind the show, J. Michael Straczynski, would doubtless argue. It is about characters and how they react to the war they are being drawn into. So it is about G'Kar feeling like an outsider and urging the others to let him become part of the War Council, the pressures that Sheridan faces in leading the alliance against the darkness, Ivanova refusing to accept defeat in her mission to persuade the First Ones to join the fight, and Delenn's feelings when she is asked to become a military leader by taking command of the Rangers. It is also about ideas, and in that regard "Ship of Tears" is a pivotal moment in the progress toward war.

"Ship of Tears" marks the gear change in Babylon 5's stand against the Shadows. Sheridan's final words in that episode, "We've got a weapon," represent a transition from being on the defensive to taking the initiative. The "weapon" he refers to is telepathy, a means to defeat the Shadows in one-to-one combat. Such an open confrontation would have been impossible prior to this point, and the shift in emphasis is underlined visually with the introduction of the war room. Babylon 5 is now very much the center of operations.

After "Ship of Tears," things begin to escalate. Sheridan persuades Kosh to bring the Vorlons into the fight in "Interludes and Examinations," which, in turn, convinces other races to join the alliance. The effectiveness of the telepathic weapon is tested by Lyta Alexander in the *White Star* in "Walkabout." And Sheridan realizes the Shadows are planning a major attack in the center of the galaxy in "And the Rock Cried Out, 'No Hiding Place.' " With all this information in place, "Shadow Dancing" delivers the confrontation—the space battle—that seemed inevitable. It is a fantastic light show, and after keeping the audience waiting all season for the showdown, *Babylon 5* would have been remiss if it neglected to deliver such a battle among the stars. But more important than the light show is the context. Here is everything that had been set up, playing out in one giant arena. The telepaths being involved in the fight, the alliance of races joining together to defeat the Shadows, and at the center of it all, Sheridan and Delenn. The battle ends, significantly, with Sheridan and Delenn looking out at a starfield littered with pieces of broken ships, and their looks of sorrow at the destruction around them emphasize the cost of war.

The revelation that telepaths have a role in the war brings together a number of plot threads that had seemed almost entirely unrelated. This one fact suddenly resonates through the earlier episodes, revealing a purpose to many aspects of the *Babylon 5* universe. Telepaths, a standard premise in science fiction, seemed just to be adding another bit of color to the series in the beginning. They provided an opportunity to tell a few good stories and, with the involvement of the Psi Corps, played a part in the conspiracies that were undermining Earth. With a rush of insight, the audience suddenly sees that they are much more. They were put there for a reason—to fight the Shadows—and they were put there by the Vorlons. This illuminates much about the Vorlons and how their manipulation of Humanity was partly to create telepaths. The key to finding out this information is G'Kar's Book of G'Quan. It explains why there are no Narn telepaths—in the previous war, they were wiped out by the Shadows—and this goes right back to the pilot when G'Kar was trying to persuade Lyta Alexander to help him breed Narn telepaths.

It also demonstrates how the other races, and Humans in particular, have been caught up in the middle of a fight between the Vorlons and the Shadows. The Psi Corps was an organization used by the Shadows to undermine Vorlon plans for the telepaths, as Shadow agent Justin confirms to Sheridan in "Z'ha'dum." This makes sense of so much that has gone before, from the Psi Corps' fanatical control over telepaths to Morden's manipulation of Earth policy with the help of a Psi Cop as seen in "Matters of Honor." Such hints are confirmed in "Ship of Tears," with Bester's acknowledgment that the Shadows are influencing Earth president Clark. Also in "Ship of Tears," Bester helps Sheridan intercept a transport of telepaths en route to join the Shadow fleet and become the living central cores of their ships. The telepathic ability genetically engineered by the Vorlons is being turned against them by the Shadows, with Humans as the pawns in the middle.

The season, therefore, sees a turnaround in the viewers' perception of the Vorlons. What began as a mysterious race that gradually revealed its secrets over the course of the first two years becomes something much darker. At the end of Season Two, Kosh emerged from his encounter suit to rescue Sheridan, revealing his angelic form to a collection of races in the Zen Garden. This image of a religious icon, the epitome of goodness, is steadily worn away as the story progresses. Even in Season Two, there was a suggestion of a dark side to the Vorlons, with their decision to send a torturer to interrogate Delenn and Sheridan in "Comes the Inquisitor" and with Kosh's angelic appearance in the Zen Garden apparently a mental projection engineered by Kosh. Season Three adds to that, with the reaction of the First Ones that Ivanova finds in "Voices of Authority"; they are angered at the very mention of the word *Vorlons*. In "Dust to Dust," G'Kar's religious visions are manipulated by Kosh, and the Narn emerges from that experience ready to join the fight—a fight engineered by the Vorlons that they themselves are reluctant to enter.

The Vorlons' position comes to a head in "Interludes and Examinations," where Sheridan confronts Kosh and demands the Vorlons take a stand in the war. Kosh's reaction is a violent one, slamming Sheridan up against the wall almost to the point of killing him. Sheridan's remark, "the real Kosh shows his colors," expresses the final transformation in the audience's perception of these aliens. They may have appeared as angels, but they are far from angelic. They are capable of violence and of anger and are happy to let others fight their war for them. And yet, at the end of this episode when Kosh is killed, the audience feels a loss. After all that has gone before, this is an intriguing reaction. The episode, in many ways, provokes this response from the viewer. Kosh's reaction to Sheridan's demand may have been violent, but he relented in the end and showed emotions that appear very Human. That is accentuated when Kosh appears as Sheridan's father in his dream. He admits having Human frailties, having been wrong, having been afraid, and this endears the audience to him, even though he is manipulating Sheridan's emotions by choosing to appear to him as someone he cares about.

With the death of Kosh, a replacement Vorlon ambassador arrives, and the contrast between the two of them completes the change in the viewers' perception of these aliens. This second Kosh is an unforgiving, malevolent creature who sets the characters on the road to reversing any sympathies they may have had with his race.

As conflict escalates through the galaxy, a crisis brews for the Humans on Babylon 5 as they are forced to make a choice between obeying their superior officers back on Earth or following their consciences. Right from the very beginning, differences between the way Babylon 5 was being run and Earth policy created tension between the two. With the arrival of Sheridan and his covert operation to expose the assassination of President Santiago by incoming President Clark, the tension increased. Then, with the arrival of Nightwatch, Babylon 5 is set on a collision course with Earth.

Episode by episode, Nightwatch's presence becomes stronger, infiltrating the space station with an increasing number of members, steadily undermining the authority of the command staff. The Ministry of Peace's attempt to install a political officer in "Voices of Authority" is averted when the crisis over President Santiago's assassination hits Earth, but it is only a temporary respite in their plans to exercise greater control over Babylon 5. The political officer leaves behind an ever-strengthening Nightwatch organization with instructions to uncover opposition to Earth, and all the foreboding resonances that has with the rise of Nazi Germany. At the same time, evidence surfaces of President Clark's associations with the Shadows. It is only a matter of time before Babylon 5 is caught in the middle.

The three episodes where the situation comes to a head—"Messages from Earth," "Point of No Return," and

"Severed Dreams"—form a pivotal point in the center of *Babylon 5*'s larger story. They see Babylon 5 break away from Earth in a move that was necessary if it were to take a decisive stand against the Shadows while Clark was still in power back on Earth. These episodes are effective because they put the characters' feelings at the heart of the story. This is a big wrench for them: many of them were born on Earth, have served Earth all their adult lives, and have always felt a sense of loyalty to their home planet. They come to realize they must reject all that if they are to follow the greater path.

Sheridan's personal crisis is dramatized when he takes the *White Star* to Earth's solar system to stop a Shadow vessel from falling into Clark's hands in "Messages from Earth." As he says in the episode, this is the closest he has been to Earth for a long time, and yet he is going in as an aggressor. He understands this is a path he must take, but it still troubles him emotionally; he finds it difficult to sleep on the journey there, and when he is faced with the prospect of firing on Earth forces for the first time, he freezes. In "Severed Dreams," just before announcing Babylon 5's independence, he takes time to call home. Here the subtext is laid bare as he talks to his father on an open channel, expressing the emotions of a man who knows it could be for the last time.

The way these episodes are structured heightens the drama, as events conspire to push Babylon 5 into a corner from which there seems to be no escape. Each time the station fights against interference from Earth, it achieves a small victory—the destruction of the Shadow vessel dug up by Earth archaeologists on Ganymede, the takeover by Nightwatch—but it is only delaying the inevitable. Even the secession from the Earth Alliance merely provokes a firefight for control of the station. This time it really seems like the end. Overwhelmed by the strength of Earth forces pitted against them, the battle appears to be lost, and only then does Delenn appear with a Minbari fleet to turn the tables and secure Babylon 5's freedom.

Another set piece for the third season is "War Without End," the two-parter that sees the temporary return of Sinclair. Sinclair had been linked into so many of the story threads that had been established in the first season that it was rewarding to see the character come back and tie them off. The questions raised by season one's "Babylon Squared," plus many other unanswered questions, made the story incredibly packed; but J. Michael Straczynski did a wise thing when he added yet more elements. The show had moved on since its Sinclair days and to have done a two-parter that concentrated only on him would have been looking backward. Instead, the episodes took the opportunity to look forward. They gave the audience a glimpse into Sheridan's and Londo's future, as well as ensuring that both the old commander—Sinclair—and the new captain—Sheridan—were given equal weight in the story.

The groundwork for Sinclair becoming Valen had been laid down since the beginning of the show, and it was fulfilling to see this plot line come full circle. It all makes sense in looking back at the earlier episodes, but few people saw it coming. The moment when it is revealed that Sinclair—the Human with the Minbari soul—is also the most influential figure to have emerged in Minbari society over the past one thousand years is a superb conclusion to the character's arc. It resolved the mystery over why Valen is referred to as "Minbari not born of Minbari," why the Grey Council released Sinclair with a twenty-four-hour gap in his memory and surrendered at the Battle of the Line, why Delenn became an ambassador on Babylon 5, and all the questions over what happened to Babylon 4. It refueled the debate among many fans over what might have happened if Sinclair had stayed, of course, but that is really a side issue. The story is as the story turned out, and "War Without End" provided the opportunity for loose ends to be tidied away. Babylon 5 could have probably continued quite happily without addressing these issues, but it is all the richer for having done so.

The glimpse of Londo in the future as an aged emperor controlled by a "keeper" on his shoulder and surrounded by his ruined home planet in "War Without End" indicates the tragic path that this character walks. He begins the season by making attempts to distance himself from Morden and turn the Centauri Republic to making its own way in the galaxy without the help of the Shadows. But all this seems for nought as events, once again, conspire to turn him into a tragic figure. When Londo turns Morden away, Refa merely takes his place, and although Londo makes inroads in separating Refa and Morden, he ends up back in the Shadows' lap himself when his beloved Adira Tyree is killed. He believes Refa is her killer, and in his quest for revenge, he goes running straight back to Morden.

What makes Londo such a tragic figure is that, at his core, he is a likeable character. This is emphasized early on in "Convictions," when Lennier saves him from an explosion that rips apart the customs area and Londo displays his gratitude by visiting him in Medlab. He does not really know what to do—in fact, there is little he can do but talk endlessly about nothing—but it is this selfless act that shows that he can care for others. That is why, when he teams up with the Shadows again, it is a tragic moment, because the audience sees that he has the potential to be a good guy.

As always, the interplay between Londo and G'Kar provides plenty of drama for the two characters. As they have effectively been separated by the war between their two peoples and G'Kar's expulsion from the Babylon 5 council, the show is forced to find new ways to bring these two together. In "Convictions," a mad bomber throws them together by trapping them in a transport tube. In "Dust to Dust," G'Kar confronts Londo inside his mind while under the influence of a drug called dust. And then, surprisingly, G'Kar and Londo move onto the same side for a brief moment to carry out Londo's plan to kill Refa in "And the Rock Cried Out, 'No Hiding Place.' " All this hints at the future path for these two characters that will end, as has been foretold, in death at each others' hands. But, as revealed in "War Without End," it seems they will die as allies and not enemies.

G'Kar's development in the third season is greater than in

any other, and at the core of his transformation is his religious experience in "Dust to Dust." The telepathic gene within him is awakened when he takes the drug dust and his mind becomes open enough to be touched by Kosh. The visions in which he faces his dying father and figures he believes to be G'Quan and G'Lan turn him onto a new path. This warrior Narn whose first thought has been for revenge is told that he can have an important role to play in the future of the galaxy if he can put that thought aside. When he emerges from that experience, he is enlightened and ready to pledge the allegiance of himself and his fellow Narns to stopping the much greater threat of the Shadows.

G'Kar had always been moving in this direction. He had been prepared to accept the hand of peace in Season Two's "The Coming of Shadows," before it was snatched away again by the Centauri attack on a Narn outpost. He'd urged the other Narns to refrain from carrying out revenge attacks on the Centauri in order to secure help for their cause in "Acts of Sacrifice." In the third season, there is a sense that he is more than just a leader to the Narns on the station and something of a teacher, particularly in "A Day in the Strife." But it is "Dust to Dust" that tips the balance. He is thrown in prison and emerges from his incarceration with a new determination.

Almost every character has an intriguing arc that spans the third season, from Zack's association with and subsequent rejection of Nightwatch, to Vir's assignment to Minbar and his growing independence. But probably one of the more significant character arcs to be played out in the third year is that which involves Franklin. His battle with stim addiction, his attempts at self-denial and facing up to the problem, had been steadily bubbling over the second year, and it eventually surfaces here. But it is his solution to the problem, to go "walkabout," that generates the most interest because he comes to address two of the central questions of the show— "Who are you?" and "What do you want?"—on a very personal level. The feeling he expresses to Garibaldi, of having lost himself by becoming embroiled in his work, is a familiar concept to the twentieth-century man who has become lost in the rat race. The metaphor of physically meeting and having a discussion with himself—(made believable because Franklin is losing blood and going into shock) brings him face-to-face with the person he is. He rediscovers himself and comes to realize that what he wants is to "do it all again." That very personal journey told over a handful of episodes is, therefore, a reflection of the greater journey taken by the galaxy as a whole, as the younger races are brought to an understanding of who they are and what they want.

While such great questions are being explored, a simple love story is unfolding between Sheridan and Delenn. This is one of the more accessible elements of *Babylon 5*, which is likely to appeal to a casual viewer. It plays with the audience with its constant teasing of when the two are actually going to realize they are fated for each other. This moment is symbolized by the kiss, forever suggested and always put off until another time . . . until "War Without End." And then what do we get? A kiss in a flashforward that may be Sheridan's first time but certainly isn't Delenn's, and the audience doesn't know whether to be satisfied or frustrated. This episode also reveals that the pair will have a son, adding another intriguing element to the love affair. The way the relationship plays out is skillfully handled, giving the audience just enough to keep viewers hooked but no more. It is an innocent love affair and, perhaps, an idealistic one but nonetheless effective for that. With so much of the show being concerned with war, conspiracies, and interpersonal conflict, it often comes as a welcome breather and helps to deepen Sheridan and Delenn's characters.

This is particularly helpful in keeping interest in Sheridan. So often the lead character is there to provide exposition and to propel the story forward and, in Sheridan's case, to be a solid military leader. That ability and his tactical mind are displayed when he encounters the Shadow vessels in "Matters of Honor" and "Messages from Earth," as well as in other situations like his confrontation with the Babylon 5 bomber in "Convictions." But even though he has this great responsibility in the third season with the encroaching Shadow War, his humanity is never far away. His relationship with Delenn, the weight of responsibility that bears down on him, and scenes like his call back home to his father all combine to keep him interesting as a character. Babylon 5's break from Earth is a personally trying time for him, but the crisis moment for Sheridan really comes in "Z'ha'dum."

The arrival of his wife shatters everything. He had put his faith in Delenn and in Kosh, and now it seems they lied to him about his wife. Not only is Anna alive and standing in his quarters, she has made a home on the Shadows' Homeworld and seems to be on the enemy's side. Sheridan had finally come to accept his wife's death, to love Delenn and make a stand against the Shadows, and it is all thrown back in his face. It emerges, of course, that Anna Sheridan has been robbed of her personality by having been placed in a Shadow ship and had previously refused to cooperate with them. Nevertheless, it marks a moment of doubt in Sheridan's mind and an important one in his development. Previously, he had accepted everything Delenn told him. Now, as he explains to her in the heat of the moment, how can he ever trust her again?

Then Sheridan, despite all the warnings, goes with Anna to Z'ha'dum. This is a defining moment for him because he almost certainly believes he will not return. He records a message for Delenn in which he explains that he is probably walking into a trap and loads the White Star with nuclear weapons that he has every intention of using. Even his last words to Garibaldi appear to be from a man who is facing death. Then, on Z'ha'dum, he follows through with his plan, bringing the White Star crashing down to the planet and exploding the nuclear weapons to devastating effect.

It would seem that Sheridan has committed the ultimate heroic act, sacrificing himself to destroy, or at least cripple, the Shadows. There seems no way he could have survived the nuclear blast, and if by some miracle he escaped by jumping off the parapet, the fall was certainly enough to kill him. This is, of course, the ultimate cliff-hanger on which to end a season. The audience is left wondering if *Babylon 5* could really have killed off its lead character. This is, after all, science fiction, and in science fiction, almost anything is possible.

Point of
No Return

Episode Guide

1
"Matters of Honor"

Cast

Captain John Sheridan	Bruce Boxleitner
Commander Susan Ivanova	Claudia Christian
Security Chief Michael Garibaldi	Jerry Doyle
Ambassador Delenn	Mira Furlan
Citizen G'Kar	Andreas Katsulas
Ambassador Londo Mollari	Peter Jurasik
Dr. Stephen Franklin	Richard Biggs
Lennier	Bill Mumy
Marcus Cole	Jason Carter
Lyta Alexander	Patricia Tallman
Vir Cotto	Stephen Furst

Guest Stars

Drazi Pilot	Jonathan Chapman
David Endawi	Tucker Smallwood
Morden	Ed Wasser
Large Man	Nils Allen Stewart
Senator	Kitty Swink
Psi Cop	Andrew Walker

Energy weapons fire at a small ship as it races away from a battle raging above Zagros 7. A shot strikes its left engine. The ship falters but manages to make it to the jumpgate intact. Inside the cockpit, Marcus Cole diverts as much power as possible from life support to the engines and heads as fast as he can to Babylon 5.

Earth has sent Mr. Endawi to the space station to find out what the other races know about a huge and powerful black spidery ship that has been seen in hyperspace. Ambassador Delenn denies any knowledge of it but afterward tells Sheridan it is a Shadow ship. "Remember it well," she says. "That is the face of our enemy."

Meanwhile, Ambassador Londo Mollari wants nothing more to do with Mr. Morden and his associates who helped the Centauri conquer the Narn. Morden agrees, on condition that Centauri forces restrict themselves to one sector of the galaxy. There is only one world on the border that Morden's associates are interested in, Zagros 7. He has asked Lord Refa to secure it for them. "Refa?" says Londo, in surprise. He suddenly looks worried.

Marcus escaped from Zagros 7 to ask Sheridan for help. He is a Ranger, one of a group of people trained to fight the Shadows, and Zagros 7 is one of their training bases. He tells Sheridan the Centauri blockade has to be broken if the other Rangers are to escape. "We have the means," he says, "if you have the will."

Marcus and Delenn take Sheridan to one of a new class of Minbari warships. It is the White Star, *a small but powerful ship that has the ability to form its own jump point, unlike most ships of its size. Sheridan takes command and heads for Zagros 7.*

The planet is worryingly quiet. There is no sign of the Centauri, and the White Star *has no problem destroying enough mines to give the Rangers a chance to escape. But they are spotted by an incoming Shadow vessel. The* White Star *evades its energy weapons and heads for the jumpgate, with the Shadow ship in pursuit. As it tracks them through hyperspace, Sheridan considers the possibility of opening a jump point inside a jumpgate. No Earth Alliance ship that has tried it has survived because it releases a staggering amount of energy. "It's suicide," Ivanova protests, but Sheridan is prepared to put his faith in the* White Star.

The White Star *heads back into normal space through a jumpgate. "Punch it!" orders Sheridan, and Lennier fires the jump engines. The two energy fields clash, sending ripples of energy through the jumpgate as the Shadow vessel follows them out of hyperspace. The energy catches the black vessel and pulls it backward, crushing it in the collapsing gate. Shock waves radiate*

out and catch up to the speeding White Star. *Power*
surges run through its instruments, and sparks shower
over the crew. They are thrown to the floor but survive.

Mr. Endawi returns to Earth and reports his
findings about the Shadow ship to an official back on
EarthDome. The only information he has is from a
thousand-year-old Narn legend. Once Endawi has left,
Morden enters, pleased by what he has overheard. He
suggests that EarthGov dismiss the sighting as an
isolated incident. But a representative from the Psi
Corps sees an advantage in perpetuating the idea of a
threat to planetary security. "There's no reason we can't
use this situation to speed up the program here at
home," he says.

The season begins with the familiar *Babylon 5* pattern of
reminding the audience of some of the main players in
the game and setting things in place for the coming year. For
the third season, this means the escalating conflict with the
Shadows, which provides the background to the personal
traumas of the main characters. The Shadow threat lies at
the heart of "Matters of Honor," which sees Sheridan face
one of their powerful ships for the first time. It also brings
Sheridan's relationship with Kosh into focus in a small scene
where Sheridan asks him about his dramatic rescue in the
Zen Garden. Meanwhile, Londo makes his first attempt to
sever ties with Morden, and a couple of new characters are
introduced.

British actor Jason Carter was brought in to play Marcus
Cole, the Ranger who comes to Babylon 5 for help and ends
up being stationed there. His first taste of working on
Babylon 5 was filming the scene in Sheridan's briefing room.
"It was my first day, and it was a big group scene," Jason
remembers. "The master shot was done, and then they were
doing close-ups, and I was the last one to have my close-up
done out of seven people. Most everybody screwed up on
their lines for some reason or other, so by the time it got to
me I knew my dialogue really well. It was easy for me, and I
did it in one or two takes. It was nice of the cast—especially

Bruce Boxleitner—to make me feel so comfortable, to know that I couldn't really fail if I could just speak my lines. It was particularly good because there was no starry attitudes going on, none of that ego power play. There was a lot of sport and joking about, which was also comfortable. I hadn't been in a working environment in America before where everyone was so nice."

Introducing a Ranger as a cast regular helped one section of the story make the transition from being in the background to being in the foreground, as writer and creator J. Michael Straczynski explains, "I thought, instead of the Ranger of the week, let's have an ongoing presence there. Marcus was meant to be that ongoing presence, as a constant reminder of who they are. If you bring in someone on an episode-by-episode basis, they are only there for the plot. With Marcus there on a permanent basis, you could do other kinds of stories and, in the process of this, learn more about what the Rangers are and what they can do."

The episode demonstrates that there is more to Marcus than being a token Ranger. Dr. Franklin's diagnosis when Marcus first arrives is that he will not be going out of Medlab for some while, but as soon as his back is turned, Marcus regains consciousness and is gone. He reveals some of his personal background, telling Ivanova how his brother was killed in the service of the Rangers and how he joined up to finish what his brother had begun. He also shows his capabilities with the Minbari fighting pike, when he extends the tube with a shake of his wrist and the help of computer graphics. "I'm particularly dextrous with it," says Jason. "I hold the pike—the short one—I take it out and continue the acting, focusing on whatever it is. Shake it. Freeze. Drop it without moving your hand, the other one gets put into place [by a member of the crew], and then carry on. Then they'll put in the extension or even throw in an edit if necessary, just to cover the stationary few moments."

The fight scene where Marcus, Delenn, and Lennier are set upon by a pair of thugs was originally going to be more elaborate, but it was cut short because of a lack of filming time. Nevertheless, it gave a rare chance for Delenn to show that Marcus is not the only one who can handle a Minbari fighting pike. "I was practicing with that stick they gave me." remembers Mira Furlan, who plays Delenn. "That's hard. I don't feel like an action heroine in any way. I was never into action movies, I'm embarrassed to say. I came from a totally different kind of background, but it's fun. I have to open myself to that. It's always fun to do onstage or in film stuff that you have problems with in life. In a way you can absolve yourself from your clumsiness in ordinary life."

In many respects, the second character to be introduced at the beginning of the third season is the *White Star*. Delenn gives it a big buildup as she leads Sheridan and Ivanova down several corridors before taking them onto the bridge. Sheridan and Ivanova are clearly impressed. "I figured it was cool; it could do some nifty stuff," says Joe Straczynski. "The problem with it for most of the third season was it was never quite right on the inside. If you look at episodes where you see it being used and take those scenes and line them up, the layout keeps changing on the interior of the *White Star*. It was never quite what I had in mind. I wanted it to be more organic looking and less prosaic."

Part of the problem with the set was that it was erected in the space reserved for the main guest set of the week. It had to be built so it could be taken down and replaced with something else whenever the need arose. (That changed in the fourth season when the *White Star* was given an overhaul and its own personal space on the soundstage.) Kevin Cremin was the director for "Matters of Honor," and he, like many who followed him, found the *White Star* problematic. "First times in prominent sets are always trouble," he says. "They're real hard on directors because you learn the little ins and outs and the best way to put a camera in *after* you've been in there a little while."

Kevin had been production manager for the previous two years and was used to being present at early production meetings. He had moved onto other projects by the third year and found it strange to come back as a freelance director. "I only came in a week and a half ahead of time because that's all the prep that a director gets, and I really felt left out of it because a lot of conversations had taken place that I wasn't present at. So, out of all the people there, I had the least idea of what this *White Star* was. I kind of garnered a little bit of information about it as we got going, but I don't think that it was a completely gelled idea yet. If I knew then what I know now, I would probably have tried to do some things a little bit differently."

The first outing for the *White Star* puts it directly in the firing line when it unexpectedly comes up against a lone Shadow vessel. Sheridan uses strategy rather than brute force to defeat it, evoking parallels to his destruction of the *Black Star* in the Earth-Minbari War. "I wanted to start showing why Sheridan got where he is," says Joe Straczynski. "He's fast on his feet. Whereas the Minbari might not be able to find a way to stop this thing, Sheridan is totally nuts and willing to take chances that the Minbari—being more rigid—would not necessarily take."

The episode ends with a final twist, where it is revealed that the Shadows have powerful friends on Earth. Three prongs of conspiracy are bought together when Morden and a Psi Cop discuss the Shadow vessel with a senator in EarthDome. The threat is tripled, and the audience's suspicions are confirmed. "You can only tease an audience for so long," says Joe. "At some point you have to put your cards on the table and say, 'Here's what's actually happening,' otherwise it gets frustrating. I thought, okay, lets take these cards and put them straight up on the deck and see what the reaction is."

2
"Convictions"

Cast

Captain John Sheridan ....Bruce Boxleitner
Commander Susan Ivanova ....Claudia Christian
Security Chief Michael Garibaldi ....Jerry Doyle
Ambassador Delenn ....Mira Furlan
Citizen G'Kar ....Andreas Katsulas
Ambassador Londo Mollari ....Peter Jurasik
Dr. Stephen Franklin ....Richard Biggs
Lennier ....Bill Mumy
Marcus Cole ....Jason Carter
Lyta Alexander ....Patricia Tallman
Vir Cotto ....Stephen Furst

Guest Stars

Robert Carlson ....Patrick Kilpatrick
Brother Theo ....Louis Turenne
Morishi ....Cary Tagawa
Drazi No. 1..Michael McKenzie
Lurker No. 1 ....Jason Larimore
Security Guard No. 1 ....Rick Johnson
Obnoxious Man ....John C. Flinn III
Woman ....Leslie Pratt
Centauri Woman ....Lorain Shields
Med. Tech. ....Gwen McGee
Security Guard No. 2 ....Tom Simmons

A bomb rips through the customs area. Lennier grabs Londo and pushes him through the door as flames leap up behind them. The pressure doors close automatically, and Lennier is trapped as another explosion shoots fire over his body.

Lennier lies in a coma in Medlab, where Londo visits him to thank him for saving his life. He is unable to do anything to help except talk in the hope Lennier's unconscious mind will hear.

Londo leaves and is about to step into the transport tube when he sees G'Kar already inside. He decides to wait for the next one. Then another explosion down the corridor makes him turn. He sees a ball of fire hurtling toward him. He dives into the transport tube as flames lick the walls where he stood.

Londo wakes up on the floor in an atmosphere of heat and smoke. A fire is raging outside the tiny compartment where he and G'Kar are trapped. G'Kar laughs. "I get to watch you die . . . I find this most appealing."

Babylon 5 staff, with a little help from Brother Theo and his order of monks, identify the bomber from video footage of the scenes of the explosions as maintenance technician Robert Carlson. Sheridan and Garibaldi prepare to storm his quarters, but one of Carlson's booby traps alerts him to their presence and he demands to see Sheridan alone.

Carlson faces Sheridan with a PPG in one hand and a trigger for the largest bomb yet in the other. "I want you to get me out of here, Sheridan," he says, "because if you don't, I'll let this go and the whole place will go up in an explosion as bright as the sun."

Garibaldi is listening outside through Sheridan's hidden link. He has a hunch that the next bomb has been attached to the fusion reactor.

Carlson is like the bombs he creates, constantly exploding in Sheridan's face, telling him how he lost his job back on Earth, lost his wife, and lost his apartment. He waves his PPG at Sheridan, telling him he wants others to know fear and to be an audience to the artistry of the bomber. He orders Sheridan to sit down, and reluctantly, Sheridan sits, putting pressure on his hidden link, which switches off with a telltale electronic bleep.

"You lied to me," says Carlson. "Just like all the

*others. To hell with all of you!" Sheridan jumps up and
dives toward him before Carlson can let go of the bomb
trigger. He punches him in the face. Carlson resolutely
keeps hold of the trigger and returns the punch. Sheridan
falls to the floor and looks up helplessly as Carlson lets
go of the trigger and it drops to the ground, sending the
signal for the bomb to explode.*

*Outside, a maintenance 'bot is taking the bomb away
from Babylon 5. It explodes in a white light and creates
a shock wave that makes the station shudder but causes
no damage. Carlson's scheme is destroyed, and he is
thrown in the brig.*

*Back in Medlab, Lennier finally regains consciousness.
Delenn tells him that Londo is grateful that he saved his
life, but Lennier wonders at the wisdom of his actions.
"I fear I have served the present by sacrificing the
future," he says.*

*Londo's life is saved a second time when a rescue
team finds him and G'Kar in the transport tube. This
time it is Londo who laughs, knowing that he is not
going to die after all. "So it would seem," says G'Kar.
"Well, it is an imperfect universe . . ."*

*B*abylon 5 isn't beyond throwing in the odd in-joke, and
there are a couple in "Convictions." In one of the early
scenes, Lennier claims to be suffering from a fictional ail-
ment, Netter's syndrome, which is an obvious reference to
the show's executive producer, Douglas Netter. Meanwhile,
the person he tells this little white lie to is the Obnoxious
Man, played by *Babylon 5*'s resident director of photography
and former actor, John C. Flinn III. "I walk into the prepping
director's office, and [producer] John Copeland's in there
with [director] Mike Vejar, and as soon as I walk in, John
Copeland says '. . . and speaking of the Obnoxious Man . . .'
and he throws me the script," John remembers. "I said,
'What is this?' and he said, 'You're it!' I said, 'What, are you
playing tag here?' and he said, 'You're it, go and learn your
lines.'

"To work with Bill Mumy was so fun," he continues. "I worked on it, and Billy says, 'I've got an idea. When you say, "I've got hair, you've got a bone," pat me on top of the head.' I didn't want to get physical with him at all because you don't do that with the Minbari! Well Christ, the place went down laughing! It was really a lot of fun, and I got a lot of responses from it."

It is a piece of light relief before the customs area is ripped apart by an explosion in a rare example, for *Babylon 5*, of on-the-set special effects. "Obviously, our quest is to make them look as if they are as dangerous as possible, without being dangerous at all," says episode director Mike Vejar. "We intercut a stunt person when he got thrown into the door to the docking bay, but Billy did part of the stuff himself. That sort of stuff is fairly simple because it is contained. Utilizing longer lenses and things like that, we can make the fire and explosions look like they're closer than they really are."

"The bomber is more or less a plot device in which I wanted to create a situation which put everyone into a pressure cooker," says writer Joe Straczynski. "We had recently had the Oklahoma City bombing [in which 168 people were killed in an explosion at a federal government building in Oklahoma], and I was very angry about that and wanted to find them and punch their lights out. Better still, if we can't do it ourselves, we can write about it. That was somewhere in the back of my head, I'm sure."

When the bomber targets Babylon 5, he not only plunges the station into crisis, he throws together characters who would otherwise remain apart. When a bomb explodes in the customs area, Lennier instinctively risks his own life to save Londo. In the midst of his increasing isolation, Londo suddenly finds someone who cares about him. The only way he can help Lennier in return is to visit him in Medlab. In reality, Londo was the only person in that scene because instead of Lennier lying in the bed there was a mannequin. Actor Bill Mumy had recently lost his father, and the thought of being in that scene was too much. "I couldn't do it," he says. "I went to them and said 'Quite honestly, I'm burying my father today, and I've just spent three months with him in a hospital lying like this. I can't do it.' They were really great about it and had this false Lennier head made up. [Makeup artist] Greg Funk said, 'Don't worry about it. I'll make this thing so no one will know the difference.' So all of those scenes in Medlab, except the one where I wake up, they're speaking to a dummy. It was a head cast, and no one knew it! It was so funny to me when I look back on it now. Andreas came in to me in the makeup room one day when he'd watched that show on the air much later, and he said to me, 'It's so difficult to just be still, and you were so focused; don't take this the wrong way, but that was some of your best work.' I just laughed and looked at him and said, 'Thank you, Andreas.' "

Another bomb throws Londo and G'Kar together, trapping them in the transport tube. So many television series have used this device that it has become something of a cliché, which is precisely why Joe Straczynski wanted to tackle it. "There is a stereotype in all television storytelling, which is to take two characters who hate each other and put them in an awful situation and they have to work together to get out of it alive, and I am *so* tired of that. I thought, let me take this old notion and turn it up on its ear to see what happens. The notion of G'Kar saying, 'No, I'm not going to help you— *die*—I don't care,' was wonderful. I can look at that piece of film endlessly, even at him singing the little fishy song, and just roll on the floor laughing."

"Everybody talks about that scene," says Andreas Kat- sulas, who plays G'Kar. "It was one of the very rare times when I worked on my part, took it very seriously, took it home and beat my brains out about how to do it. Usually, I see things very clearly, almost instantly; it's like an impulse, 'Oh, I'll play it this way' or 'I'll do it that way.' Then it hit me like dynamite that I find all of this delightfully funny. The irony of it tickles the character more than anything else, that I've got him exactly where I want him and we're both going to die. I said to Joe, 'I don't know if I can pull it off,' because laughing is harder than tears. To create genuine laughter, take after take, is hard. So I think the scene came off rather well."

The bomber is eventually tracked down by the most unlikely group of detectives, an order of monks led by Brother Theo. These characters set up base on Babylon 5 in "Convictions" and continue to make occasional appearances. "In reality, if we were to make contact with aliens who had their own belief structures, after the scientists and the researchers and the archaeologists and the builders left to go there, the next bus would have the evangelists and the religious folk," says Joe. "To find out what they believe, in case they might have a better grasp of, or a recognition of, the Almightly than we have. Or, on the flip side, to take these poor heathens and convert them to our ways. There are a number of religious folk who are big believers in inter-faith research and studies, particularly Jesuits. I thought, let's take this and deal with this, bring in these characters and have them there. They're also a kind of counterpoint to the military characters and the bad guys we tend to have on this show."

Classically, the showdown for the episode pits Sheridan in a lone standoff with the bomber. "That was really good, tense, well-written, and well-performed stuff," remembers director Mike Vejar. "Casting was very important for that character [the bomber] because that's the kind of part that can become very melodramatic and over the top, and I thought he [Patrick Kilpatrick] handled that part in such a way that you got all the craziness without making him an arch villain."

"He spat all over me," remembers Sheridan actor Bruce Boxleitner. "I was supposed to stand there very heroic, very stern, lock-jawed, 'I'm not going to take this,' and he's got this bomb, so I'm sort of tensed up, and this actor frothed all over me like a mad dog—and I stood there and went, 'Urghh!' I know it's rather gross, but these things happen."

While the episode was being filmed, the news was full of the Unabomber, who had been targeting various organizations in the United States with parcel bombs. Bruce Boxleitner remembers it led to the Carlson character being known on set as "the Unabomber of space." "He was a very excitable gentleman. He got into his part too much . . . In fact, when the Unabomber was caught, I thought we'd see *him* in the arms of the FBI!" he jokes.

3
"A Day in the Strife"

Cast

Captain John Sheridan ....Bruce Boxleitner
Commander Susan Ivanova ....Claudia Christian
Security Chief Michael Garibaldi ....Jerry Doyle
Ambassador Delenn ....Mira Furlan
Citizen G'Kar ....Andreas Katsulas
Ambassador Londo Mollari ....Peter Jurasik
Dr. Stephen Franklin ....Richard Biggs
Lennier ....Bill Mumy
Marcus Cole ....Jason Carter
Lyta Alexander ....Patricia Tallman
Vir Cotto ....Stephen Furst

Guest Stars

Troublemaker.. John St. Ryan
Na'Far ....Stephen Macht
Corwin ....Joshua Cox
Med. Tech. ....Larita Shelby
Narn No. 1 ....Neil Bradley
Dr. Gonzalez.......................................Anne Betancourt
G'Dok ....Michael Bailey Smith
Ta'Lon ....Marshall Teague
Narn No. 2 ....Mark Hendrickson

A small alien craft approaches Babylon 5, broadcasting an offer of advanced technology and cures for disease. All it requires in return is the answers to some scientific questions. If the craft doesn't receive them within twenty-four hours, it will self-destruct with enough energy to take the station with it.

Garibaldi places a basket of bread on the table in his quarters as part of the meal he has prepared for himself and Dr. Franklin. "So, why the sudden invitation to dinner?" asks Franklin. Garibaldi explains that he is worried about the amount of stims his friend has been taking. "I don't have a problem, Michael," Franklin retorts. "But if it makes you happy, I'll cut back on the stims."

Later in Medlab, Franklin finds himself yelling at a doctor back on Earth who has managed to answer most of the medical questions required by the alien probe. "You can't just give me some of them and say it's enough!" he shouts, and snaps off the transmission. He rubs the tiredness out of his eyes, but it does not do much good. He reaches into the drawer for a stim and injects it.

Vir is furious. Londo has arranged for him to become an envoy to Minbar, but Vir doesn't want to go. "I want you away from here," Londo tells him. "There are some things you shouldn't have to know or be a part of." Vir protests that Londo will be alone if he leaves. But Londo waves off his concerns. "I have always been alone," he says.

G'Kar is also being forced to leave. The Centauri are threatening to harass, imprison, or even torture the families of the other Narns on Babylon 5 unless he returns home and surrenders to them. Garibaldi begs him to stay, knowing the Centauri will kill him if he goes back. But G'Kar cannot be swayed. "My fate is in the hands of G'Quan," he says. "What must happen, will happen."

G'Kar heads toward the transport, only to be blocked by a whole corridor full of Narns. "We cannot let you leave, G'Kar," says one. "You are valued and needed here." G'Kar is touched by their concern but asks if anything can be more important than the safety of their families. "Their freedom," says another. "Better to die in the cause of freedom than live in comfort as a slave." G'Kar smiles and agrees to stay.

It is three minutes until the deadline set by the probe, and Sheridan has started to have doubts. "What if it's a berserker?" he says as the minutes slip away. "A probe whose job it is to find life-forms advanced enough to

*pose a threat to the race that created it. If it gets the
right answers, that proves a certain level of technological
advancement, and then boom!" Ivanova looks
exasperated. She has all the answers to the questions
lined up, and there is no time for a lengthy discussion.
Sheridan has to make a life-or-death decision, and he has
to make it now. "No send," he says. Tension spreads
through the Observation Dome as the seconds count
down toward the deadline. It passes. The probe turns
around and heads harmlessly away from the station.*

*Sheridan is already thinking about the probe's next
victim and orders its questions to be answered via one of
the outlying security 'bots. The probe absorbs the
information. Energy builds up inside it, until it reaches
critical and self-destructs in an explosion that floods the
Observation Dome in a brilliant white light.*

It was more than a day of strife for the crew of *Babylon 5*
when behind-the-scenes events brought the filming of this
episode to a halt. Director David Eagle remembers they were
four days into the shoot when he went back to the set after
lunch, and no one joined him. "I'm sitting on the set, and ten
minutes go by, fifteen minutes go by, twenty minutes go by,
and I'm thinking, 'Where is everybody?' " he says. "Then I
heard someone walking toward me, and it was the first
assistant director, Pam Eilerson, and she said, 'Listen, you
better come up to the front.' So I went up to the front office,
and all the people in the offices were peering out the win-
dows to see the entire crew standing out at the front of the
building. I looked to [producer] John Copeland, and I said, 'Is
this what I think it is?' and he said, 'Yep.' The crew was on
strike."

Babylon 5's film crew had always been nonunion, but by
the third season, they decided the situation should change.
"John Copeland, I must say, was really kind of the savior of
the whole situation," David Eagle continues. "He recognized
that going union was important to the crew, and in order to
continue things in harmony, it really made best sense to

settle and allow the crew to become union but to do it in a way that wouldn't put the company out of business. He was very influential, and most people don't recognize the role that he played in saving the jobs of the crew and saving the show."

Ironically, this was the episode where the fictional world of *Babylon 5* was having its own industrial-relations problem with the Transport Association. They were in dispute over new policies regarding searching incoming vessels for weapons following the escalation in the Narn-Centauri War. This small subplot was just part of the slice-of-life theme that binds the various elements of the episode together. One of these elements, Londo arranging for Vir to be sent to Minbar, was the result of another behind-the-scenes event. Actor Stephen Furst had been cast in a new sitcom, *Misery Loves Company,* and wanted to spend most of his time filming over at Disney's studios. "It was quite a bit of money, and it was also a chance to break out and become more well-known," says Stephen.

Joe Straczynski took it in stride, as always, and saw real life's input into the show as an opportunity rather than a problem. "Vir going off to Minbar because Stephen was going off to *Misery Loves Company* gave me the opportunity to further isolate Londo," says the writer. "In the course of the three years he was losing friends, acquaintances, he and Garibaldi weren't talking very much anymore, and by removing Vir, it removed one more layer of comfort for Londo. So actually, it served very well for the story."

On one level, the various story threads work to produce a stand-alone episode that is designed to ease new viewers into the characters and situations at the beginning of a season. On another, it inches the story forward in ways that don't reveal their significance until later. That is particularly so in the scene in which Garibaldi visits G'Kar in his quarters and asks him not to go back to Narn where he will most likely be killed. In the context of the episode, the scene serves to emphasize the danger G'Kar will face and the calm manner in which he faces that danger. In the context of the story as a whole, it is no accident that Garibaldi is the one to visit G'Kar to persuade him to reconsider. This is the beginning of a relationship that grows through the season.

For Andreas Katsulas, who plays G'Kar, the relationship was totally unexpected. "I don't know why those two hit it off well, as opposed to he and Dr. Franklin," he says. "How does G'Kar know that Garibaldi is any different from anyone else? It's like visiting someone in the hospital; it seems like nothing, but if you don't do it, you don't show how you feel. So here comes Garibaldi who's concerned about him, and this isn't wasted on G'Kar. No one else has come to see how G'Kar is doing and why he's leaving, so this is a check mark for Garibaldi in G'Kar's heart."

The ones who are able to persuade him to stay are the other Narns. Their faith in him, and his doctrine to resist the Centauri whatever the cost, is what leads them to sacrifice the safety of their families for the greater cause. "I'm in a little bit of a quandary, even after having done it," admits Andreas Katsulas. "I'm still not sure what it all means. There's this thing that Joe keeps setting up of 'Have you learned no better than this?' where he's almost speaking to them as a spiritual teacher would, and yet the groundwork for that has never been established. In other words, we haven't seen him—whether it's in a religious sense or in a sense that he is their teacher—that he could ask, 'Have you learned no better?' Unless he simply means, 'Has life taught you no better? Aren't you aware as I am? Aren't you transforming along with me? Aren't you seeing this?' But why should they? He's had a very special series of situations that have allowed him to develop this way."

There is a sense in which G'Kar, as the last surviving member of the ruling Kha'Ri, is leading his people onto the next level of their development. His lesson in Season Two's "Acts of Sacrifice" was that short-term sacrifice is sometimes necessary to achieve a long-term goal. In that episode, he told them not to seek immediate revenge against the Centauri but to act in a manner that would encourage other races to help their side. Here his lesson is reflected back at him, as the other Narns sacrifice the immediate safety of their families to achieve their long-term freedom. Alongside this is G'Kar's personal journey that has taken him from the warlike being of Season One to the person who will ultimately bring his people back from the brink of despair. Ultimately, his writings will become known as the Book of G'Kar and be followed, just as he follows the Book of G'Quan. At this point, however, G'Kar no more knows his fate than the actor who portrays him.

Franklin is facing a much more personal crisis as Garibaldi confronts him about his use of stims. Franklin clearly has a problem, but he is not ready to admit it. "I did a little research on addiction, and there are certain stages that everyone goes through, and the first is denial," says actor Richard Biggs. "You deny that you have a problem, then it progresses. There's guilt, and then you finally accept it. Once you accept it, that's the first stage if you're going to change."

What makes Franklin's addiction more interesting, dramatically, is that it is the reformed alcoholic—Garibaldi—who challenges him about it. "I've been there, done that, got the T-shirt," as Jerry Doyle, who plays Garibaldi, puts it. "I think if you are a friend—and I believe the characters are friends, good friends—sometimes you have to have the tough conversations with your friends. It's easy to have nice fluffy conversations with acquaintances, but sometimes with friends you've got to give them reality checks, you have to give the wake-up calls, you have to call people on their bullshit, you have to make them realize what they're doing to themselves or others. This is one of those situations."

While these personal crises are being tackled throughout the station, Babylon 5 is facing a crisis of its own. The probe acts as a framing device into which all the other elements fit, even though, for the most part, they don't relate to it. It is very much like the real world, where personal lives continue while greater events shape the world around us. The space station can be a dangerous place, and the day the probe arrived was just another day in the life of Babylon 5.

4

"Passing Through Gethsemane"

Cast

Captain John Sheridan	Bruce Boxleitner
Commander Susan Ivanova	Claudia Christian
Security Chief Michael Garibaldi	Jerry Doyle
Ambassador Delenn	Mira Furlan
Citizen G'Kar	Andreas Katsulas
Ambassador Londo Mollari	Peter Jurasik
Dr. Stephen Franklin	Richard Biggs
Lennier	Bill Mumy
Marcus Cole	Jason Carter
Lyta Alexander	Patricia Tallman
Vir Cotto	Stephen Furst

Guest Stars

Brother Edward	Brad Dourif
Brother Theo	Louis Turenne
Businessperson	Natalie Brunt
News Anchor No. 1	Steven Gonzales
Centauri	Mark Folger
News Anchor No. 2	Lynn Blades
Man	Robert Keith
Security Guard No. 2	Thomas Mills

Lyta Alexander emerges from Kosh's ship, having returned from the Vorlon Homeworld. "Nobody's ever been to the Vorlon Homeworld and back again," Garibaldi later comments to Sheridan, Ivanova, and Franklin. "Is anybody else as creeped out about this as I am?" All three raise their hands.

Brother Edward, a monk from Theo's order, is visiting Delenn and Lennier to find out more about the Minbari religion. In return, Delenn wants to know the emotional core of his faith. Edward relates the story of Jesus at the garden of Gethsemane, where he waited for the soldiers to come, even though he knew they would take him to his death. "I've often thought about that night," says Edward, "and I honestly don't know if I would have had the courage to stay."

Edward hears a woman's scream in the corridor near his quarters and runs toward the sound. But there is no one there. A sudden pain shoots through his mind, and other noises cloud his head. Voices. Whispering. "Charlie . . . You killed her, Charlie . . ." He sees a message scrawled on the wall in blood, "Death walks among you." Edward turns, disoriented and confused. He runs, and instead of his feet hitting the hard floor, they splash through water. He stumbles, falling facedown in it. Dripping, he turns to see a woman lying beside him. She is dead, and in her mouth is a black rose.

Edward doesn't know if the things he has seen are real or imagined and asks the computer to search Earth records. It retrieves an ISN news report on Charles Dexter, the Black Rose Killer. Edward freezes the footage as it shows Dexter being led out of court. He finds himself staring at his own face, the face of a murderer.

Dexter was sentenced to the "death of personality"; his mind was wiped and replaced with a new personality that was programmed to serve society. "Do you know what it's like to wake up one day and find out you're a monster?" Edward asks Theo.

Edward leaves the order to seek justice for his sins. He is praying when he senses a group of people approaching. He looks up to face the sons, daughters, and husbands of the women he murdered. "I knew you would come," he says, masking his fear with dignified calm.

The victims' families had used a Centauri telepath to break down Edward's mindwipe. They wanted him to remember what he had done before administering their own form of justice. Garibaldi arrests the Centauri and, with the help of Lyta's telepathic skills, finds out where Edward is. Garibaldi, Sheridan, and Theo find Edward, battered and bloody, hanging from a metal grill in Brown 42, but it is too late. "I always wondered if I would have had the courage to stay at the garden at Gethsemane," says Edward as his life slips away. "Now I know."

Sheridan is in the Zen Garden with Brother Theo, reflecting on what happened to Edward. "Where does revenge end and justice begin?" he wonders. His thoughts are interrupted by a monk whom Theo introduces as a new member of the order. Sheridan recognizes Edward's killer, now mindwiped and with a new personality. He cannot hide his hatred and anger. But under Theo's stare, he shakes the man's hand and wishes him well. Forgiveness is a hard thing.

Lyta faces Kosh in his quarters. She, without her breathing mask. He, without the headpiece of his suit. Gills flex on the side of her neck, and a white, glowing energy flows from her eyes and mouth into Kosh's suit.

The story for "Passing Through Gethsemane" was originally planned for the second season but was delayed when someone innocently posted a similar idea on the computer Internet, thus causing problems over copyright. After a lot of wrangling, the matter was sorted out, and the story was resurrected to make a strong stand-alone episode for the early part of season three.

The idea of the mindwipe had been introduced in season one's "The Quality of Mercy," when Talia Winters is asked to scan a murderer in preparation for his "death of personality." That episode touched on some of the issues raised, but they were not fully scrutinized until this episode. The advantages of this punishment are clear to a late-twentieth-century Western society where prisons are overcrowded, prisoners are expensive to keep, and there is a debate about the effectiveness of sending people to jail. An alternative penalty for heinous crimes is the death penalty, but the moral questions that arise from that are even more problematic. The mind-wipe seems, at first glance, to solve all of these problems. It is cheap and rehabilitates the criminal into a useful member of society. Brother Edward is the perfect example of its success.

But it is a success that has moral implications. The mind-wipe may preserve someone's body, but isn't destroying someone's personality the same as killing him? And if the criminal is allowed to forget his crimes and continue to live, can a mindwipe really be said to be a punishment? The people who lost loved ones at Dexter/Edward's murderous hands clearly believe not. Even Edward, in his new person-ality, feels he has been denied a chance to atone for his sins.

"I wanted to pose that moral question to the audience," says writer Joe Straczynski. "Which is preferable, killing someone or using someone in a whole new life? And if you do that, what is the liability or the responsibility of the person who did commit these crimes? Is justice really served if someone is happy, leading a life somewhere thinking he's someone else and never knowing he did these things? What happens if—God forbid—that person should run into a victim or a victim's family member? It's a very sticky moral and ethical issue, therefore, I loved it a lot because there isn't a clear way to finding the answers."

The choice of putting a devout monk at the center of these questions gives them an extra dimension. There is a clear dramatic contrast between the killer he once was and the spiritual man he has become, and Edward's religious beliefs give him a different insight into his situation. For him, the question of atoning for his sins is central to his way of life, so he is devastated when he discovers his life has been built on a lie. He wonders how he can ask God to forgive his sins when he does not know what they are?

The episode asks the viewer to sympathize with Edward, when it could just as easily have asked the viewer to sympa-thize with his victims' families. Edward's torture and death provide the justice the victims' families have strived for, while the audience views them as an injustice. Sheridan feels a sense of loss when Edward is killed, and when he is introduced to Brother Malcolm, Edward's mindwiped killer, his immediate response is anger and hatred. But Malcolm is, in reality, no different from Edward. Both were killers in the past and have been turned into virtuous men. The irony of the situation merely adds another complexity to the mind-wipe debate.

While these great questions are being posed, Edward is taking a very personal and spiritual journey. It is expressed through the Christian story of Jesus at the garden of Gethsemane. At the beginning, Edward wonders if he could ever have the courage of Christ at Gethsemane. By the end, he answers his own question by having the courage to face his victims' families, knowing they will avenge the terrible things he did to their loved ones. He comes full circle, and with his death, he feels that justice will be served and he can face God.

This is one of many examples of religion and religious belief that continue to be expressed throughout *Babylon 5*. Joe Straczynski keeps returning to the theme, and there is a sense in which he is fascinated by it. "I'm not sure if I'm fascinated by religion or religious impulse," he says. "The religious impulse is the flip side of science. Both are attempts to find out where we came from, how we got here, who we are, where we're going. They both use different methodologies, but the impulse is the same. And I use the show to explore the sense of wonder, the exploration, the scientific parts of science fiction, and my feeling is 'Why not give voice to, or explore, the other side as well?' I am an atheist. I have no religious interest personally at all, but as a writer, it can lead to some very compelling drama."

Brad Dourif played Brother Edward, and for many of the cast, this is what they enjoyed about working on the episode, Bill Mumy among them. "Brad Dourif was just great," says the actor who plays Lennier. "Mira and I had very little to do in that episode, but both of us felt ourselves really coming up a notch when we were working with him. We have a great cast and we're not lazy, but a certain caliber of actor or a certain caliber of musician brings your playing up a little. And I really liked working with Brad; he was a sweet guy and did a great job . . . In fact, there's an outtake from that. We did this take, and it was really good and everything, and then Brad said, 'Someday I'd like to hear more about Val-len.' I said, 'No, no, it's *Valen*!' It was pretty funny."

The subplot sees the welcome return of Lyta Alexander, played by Patricia Tallman, now working for Kosh. She is no longer bound by Psi Corps rules, which gives her an advantage that she uses when determining Edward's whereabouts by probing a Centauri telepath. It was Pat Tallman's first appearance on *Babylon 5* since the previous year's "Divided Loyalties," and she was still breast-feeding her baby. "I don't know if you know anything about breast-feeding, but you feed the baby in the morning, and then everything swells up, your chest swells up," she says. "I have this sweater that crisscrosses in the front, and I had to lean over, and I was worried about my rear end because I still hadn't lost all the baby fat from having a baby. And I leaned over, and they're setting up the shot, and they all went, 'Woah! What a great angle!' And before I know it, Kim is running over from wardrobe sewing it up so that my boobs don't pop out! I'm going, 'No, no don't! I finally have cleavage; don't sew it up!' "

In the context of the scene, Garibaldi throws a blanket over the Centauri's head to disorient him while Lyta performs her telepathic probe. "This was another time we were trying to figure out 'when do I scan and when do I get exhausted?' " says Pat. "I'm acting with an actor who's covered in black cloth—it's not like I'm getting anything back! We were figuring out our cue as to how he would know when to collapse and when I would collapse at the same time. We laugh about it now, but when you're doing this you want to make it as real as possible, of course. It's important to the scene, and we don't make fun of it. We are really serious, but we make fun of things later just because we make fun of life."

The episode concludes with Lyta paying a visit to Kosh, and the questions posed about her earlier suddenly take on a greater significance. How could she have gone to and from the Vorlon homeworld so easily? How, after making such a physically traumatic journey, could all her previous health problems have disappeared? Now she has gills and energy is being transferred from her to Kosh's encounter suit, and the audience senses there is a difference between the woman who left for Vorlon space and the woman who has returned.

5

"Voices of Authority"

Cast

Captain John Sheridan	Bruce Boxleitner
Commander Susan Ivanova	Claudia Christian
Security Chief Michael Garibaldi	Jerry Doyle
Ambassador Delenn	Mira Furlan
Citizen G'Kar	Andreas Katsulas
Ambassador Londo Mollari	Peter Jurasik
Dr. Stephen Franklin	Richard Biggs
Lennier	Bill Mumy
Marcus Cole	Jason Carter
Lyta Alexander	Patricia Tallman
Vir Cotto	Stephen Furst
Zack Allan	Jeff Conaway

Guest Stars

Draal	John Schuck
Julie Musante	Shari Shattuck
Corwin	Joshua Cox
President Clark	Gary McGurk
First Security Guard	James Black
ISN Anchor	Vimi Mani

Julie Musante from Nightwatch breezes into Sheridan's office and announces, "I'm to be your new political officer." Sheridan is furious that this civilian from the Ministry of Peace wants jurisdiction over his station. But she is determined to make sure that he sticks to government policy.

Ivanova, meanwhile, takes up Draal's invitation to visit the planet below Babylon 5 and try using the Great Machine to locate the First Ones, ancient races who helped defeat the Shadows a thousand years ago. Ivanova enters Draal's Great Machine and allows her mind to become part of the universe. She finds herself in open space and fights for breath but, with the help of Draal's soothing words, calms herself and follows the path to the First Ones. She races through space to a planet called Sigma 957. Her mind wallows in the wonder of it all, until she senses something coming from the depths of space and is gripped by terror. "It is the enemy," says Draal. "Pull away!" Ivanova struggles and suddenly whips away, speeding back through space and seeing . . . an image from the past. It is EarthForce 1 before it exploded and killed President Santiago.

Ivanova locks onto a video image of the then vice president Clark. "I've wanted Santiago dead for so long," he says. "I wasn't sure we could really pull it off." The message is the evidence they have been searching for to prove Clark conspired to kill Santiago and take the presidency for himself.

Julie Musante tells a Nightwatch meeting that people will soon be purged from government positions on charges of sedition, immoral conduct, and spying for alien governments. Zack Allan is just one of the Nightwatch personnel shocked at the new policies, but Musante insists they are necessary. "With our basic freedoms at stake, no response can be too extreme," she says.

G'Kar accosts Garibaldi in the corridor, suspicious about all the secret meetings that have been taking place without him. "Something is going on, Mr. Garibaldi. I sense a gathering of forces that could perhaps help my people." Garibaldi denies it, but G'Kar doesn't believe him. "Perhaps I could help you," he suggests, but Garibaldi doesn't see how.

Ivanova approaches Sigma 957 with Marcus in the White Star. A giant black ship with swirling colored lights emerges out of deep space, and a glowing face materializes on the bridge of the White Star. Ivanova tells the First Ones she wants their help in the new war against the Shadows. "Zog," answers the face, and fades away.

That is the wrong answer as far as Ivanova is

concerned. She opens a com channel and begins a verbal onslaught directed at the First Ones. "The Vorlons said you wouldn't be up to a fight like this. The Vorlons said that in the last war they carried you . . . ," The glowing face rematerializes, angry but willing to take up the fight. They will be there when the time comes.

The scandal over President Clark has hit Earth, and Julie Musante has been recalled to deal with the problem. But the Nightwatch maintains its presence on the station, and it is creating an uneasiness between Garibaldi and Zack. "Nightwatch says the only people who have to worry are the ones with something to hide," says Zack. "You got something to hide, Chief?" They part on troubled terms.

Garibaldi is woken up by someone at the door to his quarters. He pulls himself out of bed and finds G'Kar, standing at the door. He hands him the Book of G'Quan. "I told you I could help . . . Read it." Garibaldi protests that he can't read Narn. "Learn!" G'Kar retorts, and heads off down the corridor.

"Voices of Authority" is full of humor. Its subject matter may deal with long-term threats to the galaxy, but it is all treated with a light touch. Draal steps out of the Great Machine on Epsilon 3, brushing himself off and saying he should dust himself once in a while. Ivanova makes an unannounced appearance in Sheridan's quarters just as the Nightwatch woman, Julie Musante, attempts to seduce him by stripping naked. And Marcus has plenty of fun at Ivanova's expense, at one point suggesting he should put a bucket on his head and pretend to be the ancient Vorlon god Boogee!

Joe Straczynski thinks he must have been struck down with a bug at the time that, as with Season One's "The Quality of Mercy," made his writing come out a little "goofy," "Every so often a little switch gets flipped in my brain, and it says, 'Let's have some fun and be nuts.' "

One of Joe's favorite lines is when Ivanova regards the naked Musante and comments to Sheridan, "I think you're about to go where *everyone* has gone before." "It's one of those lines where you think, 'I've got to use that, or I'm going to explode!' Every so often the writer says, 'Screw the show, screw the producer, just put the funny line in because it's funny.' "

When Ivanova and Marcus engage the First Ones in what is a potentially dangerous situation, Marcus's response is not fear or heroism or cunning, it is sarcasm. "I love it," says actor Jason Carter. "It's the British humor that Joe can write, the kind of *Blackadder* line. When you think about *Fawlty Towers*, it's exactly the same thing as when he's talking about his wife in obscene terms.

"I like the absolute familiarity and the disregard for structures of authority that Marcus has," he continues. "Structures of authority don't mean very much to him. The Minbari training is much more akin to martial arts and the spiritual aspects to life. Whereas Ivanova's world is a much more structured world. That's how Marcus perceives her world to be, and that's how she behaves. He doesn't understand why she cannot step beyond the mask of authority."

It is the beginning of a testy relationship between the two. There is clearly some attraction from Marcus's side, but Ivanova doesn't really know how to deal with it. It reflects the uncertainties of life, where relationships do not come in neat little packages, and there is a sense in which Joe Straczynski is playing with the relationship. Even the actors did not know where it was leading. "I don't have a clue; don't ask me," Claudia Christian commented while filming Season Four. "I swear I don't know anything. I ask about it all the time; I don't get any succinct answers from anybody."

Conversely, an actor will often have direct input on the way his or her character develops. Joe Straczynski has an office on the set, which allows the writer and actors to talk to each other about the show. Bill Mumy, for example, suggested that Lennier was in love with Delenn during the second season, and this suggestion became part of his character. In this episode, Jeff Conaway was surprised to find his off-the-cuff remarks about his jacket becoming part of the show when his character, Zack Allan, makes a play for Julie

Musante, the blonde, blue-eyed woman from Nightwatch. "Every time I looked at myself in the mirror, I looked like I was a fifty-year-old man with a beer belly," he laughs. "Whenever you moved, the thing [jacket] would pouch out. One time Bruce and I were talking, and I said, 'Have you noticed we all look fat in these jackets?' and we went in to do a scene and all of a sudden Bruce screwed up on his lines, and he turned to me and said, 'I was thinking about the jacket!' I guess they heard me talking about it or something, and all of a sudden it was in the episode!"

Zack had been a constant presence in *Babylon 5* since the middle of the second season, but his part remained small for a long time. He was just one of the station personnel happy to join up with Nightwatch. "People often get into predicaments, and they don't know how they got there," says Jeff. "They were just seemingly innocently walking along with the herd, and they end up in the slaughterhouse. I think that is what kind of happened to him; it was a little easy money and he was just doing what he was doing anyway, then when it got a little more sticky, about turning people in, his morals, his ethics, his personal self started questioning it."

Zack is not ready to go with his conscience just yet, but the tension is beginning to show, and inevitably, he clashes with Garibaldi. After so many guest appearances for Zack, this was the beginning of his taking on a more significant role. "For an actor, whenever you have something that means something, you can sink your teeth into it and play different levels. A little bit of emotion, a little bit of confrontation, with the relationship that had been building between Garibaldi and Zack and the trust factor. It was fulfilling. It was satisfying to get out and really do a real scene, not 'Who do you want me to kill?', 'Go kill a Narn,' 'Okay, I'll be right there!' " He laughs.

The hypocrisy of the Nightwatch is emphasized by Julie Musante. She claims that the crimes on Earth are committed only by deranged people; there is no homelessness and no poverty—or, at least, there is none since the Ministry of Peace rewrote the dictionary. In this discourse with

Sheridan, she shows she is intelligent enough to know what is really going on but still happy to promote Nightwatch policies. The parallel with Nazi Germany was consciously made by Joe Straczynski. "There is a process by which fascist organizations take root. They begin with genuine and very valid concerns. In Nazi Germany, before it became Nazi Germany, the nationalist party dealt with the question of unemployment, of the economy falling apart; they lightly feathered the question of outsiders being responsible for some of this. By addressing issues that people can agree with, you pull them in. Gradually, over time, the agendas become less clear cut, and they begin putting in elements that you may have not agreed with in the past and may not currently agree with, but you've already invested time and energy and personality into the organization and believed in it and it becomes harder to pull out. That begins the process of sucking you in further and further, until you can't pull out anymore without being perceived as a traitor. The Nightwatch began that way and gradually gets more and more into a repressive organization, a thought-police kind of organization, and we see Zack's growing discomfort at that."

The untimely arrival of the woman from Nightwatch gives Ivanova a chance to get out of the station for a while and become part of Draal's machine on Epsilon 3. His comment that she discovers more than a "normal" Human mind should be able to is not lost on attentive viewers who remember that Ivanova is a latent telepath. "I enjoyed that when I was in the machine, when they had that whole Joan of Arc shot of me, like really tight close-up," says actress Claudia Christian. "I thought it was pretty cool. The CGI was neat, because they went into my eyeball. I liked that episode, actually."

The sequence also picks up a bead of information from the first season's "Mind War." When Ivanova discovers the First Ones, it is at Sigma 957, the same planet where Catherine Sakai was nearly killed. This whole story begins the process of weaving together disparate threads that will be developed over the course of the season: the Great Machine, the First Ones, Clark's assassination of President

Santiago, and the changing of the audience's perception of the Vorlons, which begins when the First Ones are angered by the mention of their name. Marcus may make a joke out of it, but the First Ones' reaction makes a small contribution to the nagging doubt that the Vorlons may not be as benevolent as they would like to appear.

6
"Dust to Dust"

Cast

Captain John Sheridan	Bruce Boxleitner
Commander Susan Ivanova	Claudia Christian
Security Chief Michael Garibaldi	Jerry Doyle
Ambassador Delenn	Mira Furlan
Citizen G'Kar	Andreas Katsulas
Ambassador Londo Mollari	Peter Jurasik
Dr. Stephen Franklin	Richard Biggs
Lennier	Bill Mumy
Marcus Cole	Jason Carter
Lyta Alexander	Patricia Tallman
Vir Cotto	Stephen Furst

Guest Stars

Shop Owner	S. Marc Jordan
Bester	Walter Koenig
Security Guard No. 1	Harry Hutchinson
Crazed Man	Walter Winston O'Neil
Med. Tech.	Gwen McGee
Vizak	Kim Strauss
Lindstrom	George Gerdes
Ashi	Philip Moon
Man	David Shark
Centauri Diplomat	John-Frederick Jones
Morden (in flashback)	Ed Wasser
Narn Image	Jim Norton
Ombuds	Dani Thompson
Psi Cop	Judy Levitt

A crazed man staggers through Down Below. He sinks to his knees, screaming, "Make it stop! Make it stop!" Soon after, he is in Medlab, another victim of dust.

Dust is a drug that enhances the latent telepathic gene

in most Humans, allowing them to invade someone else's mind in an intense and highly addictive way. The Psi Corps believe that one of the main distributors of dust has come to Babylon 5, and Psi Cop Bester has come to track him down.

Bester and Garibaldi pull in a suspect for interrogation. The man says he never touches dust, but Bester—pumped with sleepers by Dr. Franklin to subdue his telepathic talent and prevent unauthorized scans— says he's lying. The suspect is so terrified of what else the Psi Cop might find in his brain that he admits he met the dust smuggler. Garibaldi regards Bester suspiciously, wondering if the sleepers really worked. "The odds were good that he was lying about something," Bester says nonchalantly. "The badge and the uniform do have certain advantages . . . Just like your badge and your uniform."

Dust could be the perfect weapon for G'Kar. Easy to smuggle in and conceal, it could be used to learn the Centauris' secrets and destroy them from the inside. There are no longer any Narn telepaths, and the drug dealer warns G'Kar that Narns may not have the relevant telepathic gene. "It's never been tested on Narns," he says. "It may have unpredictable results."

Bester and Garibaldi crouch behind some crates in the cargo bay with their PPGs ready. They watch as two sets of men arrive and exchange briefcases. "Now!" Garibaldi yells into his link, and a piercing whine engulfs the cargo bay. The dealers clamp their hands to their ears. Some try to run; others reach for their PPGs. There is an exchange of fire. Two fall down, injured, and the rest surrender. Garibaldi opens one of the briefcases to find hundreds of small packets of dust.

G'Kar—his eyes jet black from the effects of dust— stares down at Londo. His body lies slumped on the floor, bloody and bruised from where G'Kar has beaten him. G'Kar looks deeper, entering Londo's mind. He finds memories of Morden and their conspiracy to destroy the Narn. "It was you," says G'Kar. Enraged, he rips through Londo's mind, pulling out image after image.

A voice stops him, and G'Kar turns to see the image of his father. He is back on Narn, hanging from a tree, dying. Then, just as G'Kar reaches out to him, the tree disappears, and an old Narn appears beside him. "You cannot see the battle for what it is," says the vision. "We must realize we are not alone. We rise and fall together, and some of us must be sacrificed if all are to be saved." There is the sound of the flapping of wings, and G'Kar turns to see G'Lan. G'Kar watches in awe as the white, glowing, winged Narn rises into the darkness. Then he is back in the room with Londo, all dust purged from his system. Unseen by either of them, Kosh watches from the doorway.

G'Kar is sent to prison for sixty days, and with the dust smugglers captured, there is no reason for Bester to stay. Another Psi Cop joins him for the journey home. "I always said this whole dust idea wasn't going to work," Bester comments as they walk away. "We spent five years developing this stuff, tying it into latent genes, and it hasn't produced one telepath of acceptable strength."

Dust, which began as just a background detail in *Babylon 5*, becomes a catalyst for the larger story in this episode. G'Kar had no idea what it would lead to when he attempted to buy some of the drug from a dealer. His original thought was to use it as a weapon, which could be easily smuggled back to Narn to use against the Centauri. He takes some only to test its effectiveness, but as soon as he tastes its power, his thoughts turn to Londo.

"Putting Londo and G'Kar together when they had not been much together before was part of the goal with this," says Joe Straczynski. "To flip them back and forth in preying on each other. These two characters are linked at the hips whether they want to be or not. Londo victimized G'Kar; now G'Kar has a chance to turn it around."

It is difficult to imagine any similar scene in a non—science fiction drama. In the mainstream, one character might use physical or psychological methods to extract information from another character, but dust gives G'Kar the unparalleled power to take what he wants from Londo's mind. It leaves Londo totally helpless and exposed. "Andreas and I got into long discussions with Joe Straczynski about the nature of getting into Londo's mind," says Peter Jurasik, who plays Londo. "Andreas and I were rehearsing stuff together at his house, so we were working on that and trying to make that view into Londo's mind work.

"I remember feeling like I overplayed some stuff in it, which didn't work," Peter continues. "I felt when Londo gets beat up by G'Kar that the true essence of who the individual is would emerge, but I kind of forgot that and should have leaned a little harder on keeping up a good face. It's an interesting and challenging episode, but I'm not sure if it was one that worked for me."

In visual terms, the scenes had to put across the feeling of being in Londo's (and subsequently G'Kar's) mind. Exactly how this was going to be achieved was the subject of a great deal of discussion, as director David Eagle remembers: "When we were inside G'Kar's mind, the idea was that in every shot, except one, we would be in limbo, in black, in nothingness, even if it meant him kind of floating in the air in one of those shots. And popping around, in front of and behind Londo. I kind of took that whole scene and was influenced very much by a British television show from the sixties, *The Prisoner*. There was an episode called 'A, B and C.' It was done very much like this, in limbo, in black. He'd turn around and somebody would be there, and he'd turn around again and someone else would be there. That had a lot of influence on me, and it's kind of what I thought about when I was planning that particular show."

The glimpse into Londo's mind shows the transition from the man he was to the man he will become. When Londo was first sent to *Babylon 5*, his position was considered a joke, but then his dealings with Morden helped shape the galaxy, and in the future he sees himself rising to the position of emperor. On one level the scene informs G'Kar, while on another it forces Londo to review his own life. He is in a reflective mood after his ordeal and tells Vir that his position on Minbar should never be considered a joke back home. Peter Jurasik confesses to being responsible for a continuity error in that scene, which only a very observant viewer is likely to spot. "I squinted my right eye closed [in the long shot] as though he had beat me up on my right eye, and when we did my close-up, I squinted my left eye! Fans can check that and see if I'm squinting the wrong eye."

The revelations are taken one step further for G'Kar, as his attention moves away from Londo and turns back in on himself. The drug allows him to explore his own mind and bring him face-to-face with the people who have shaped his life and his beliefs. "Suddenly he has his own revelations," says Andreas Katsulas, who plays G'Kar. "All I believe in is there. It's a confrontation. It's sort of like a realization of what was [previously] just imaginary, suddenly crystalized, speaking in a voice and telling you, 'This is the path to take.' Nobody knew what effect this drug would have on a Narn. Thankfully, it had this effect on G'Kar, to sweeten his experience. He suspected there's a different way to be in life, to get a different result, but he's seen only the surface of it. Now, suddenly, he has a taste of the inner workings of that new possibility. I love the scene right before he goes to jail, after he's convicted. He gives the book to Garibaldi and says, 'I don't think I need it anymore; I'm closer to the source.' That's what I'm talking about—the experience. It's not just reading words and thinking about what they mean—he's got the experience, he knows what those words mean now."

As the conclusion of this sequence reveals, much of what G'Kar saw within his own mind was manipulated by Kosh. The Vorlon takes advantage of the altered state of G'Kar's mind to influence his development for the coming struggle, and this is reminiscent of the way he touched Sheridan in his dream in "All Alone in the Night." "It was *the* moment in G'Kar's transformation," explains Joe Straczynski.

"It's his Gandhi moment, if you will. There is the notion that for one to achieve the transformational moment, it has to come through great pain. I really had to get him and Londo and tear them all apart a little bit to get at the kernel of their personalities. That definitely was the case with G'Kar there."

The episode also sees the return of Bester, played with an evil air by Walter Koenig. But here the audience gets a different perspective on the villain from Psi Corps. For once his goal is the same as that of Sheridan, Garibaldi, and the others, to catch the dust smugglers. In the context of this episode, their reaction to him seems almost like paranoia. Bester takes the sleepers willingly and teams up effectively with Garibaldi. Joe Straczynski insists that this makes him no less of a villain, merely a more complex one. "Bester's intentions are the same now as they always have been, which is that telepaths should be running the whole operation," he says. "You often hear about even murderers having decent family lives. Hitler was a snappy dresser and a good dancer, had good fashion sense, but he was a monster, and the monster never sees a monster in the mirror. That's my first and foremost rule. It was a chance to show some additional colors to Bester but not contradictory colors. He would still do exactly the same things now that he would have done six months before. He is completely pathological, and he will appear to us as whatever will do him the best good."

That is emphasized in the penultimate scene where Bester comments to his fellow Psi Cop that dust was a drug developed by the Psi Corps. "Joe did an interesting thing," says actor Walter Koenig. "He [Bester] had a final speech that showed I was fooling them. Joe said, 'That's the way we keep Bester looking like he's not too easily conned by events.' I thought it was good that the reason I said I was there was not the real reason why I was there."

"I was in the position of knowing full well that Bester, because he had been beaten the last couple of times he was there, had the potential of becoming less of a bad guy and more of a comic foil," adds Joe. "I decided that the next time we saw him he either had to be right or he had to win, and here he did both. At the end, his own people were responsible for dust in the first place and [the audience thinks,] 'What a monster, what a creep!' You start to kinda like him, then you find that out, and you want to slug him!"

7
"*Exogenesis*"

Cast

Captain John Sheridan	Bruce Boxleitner
Commander Susan Ivanova	Claudia Christian
Security Chief Michael Garibaldi	Jerry Doyle
Ambassador Delenn	Mira Furlan
Citizen G'Kar	Andreas Katsulas
Ambassador Londo Mollari	Peter Jurasik
Dr. Stephen Franklin	Richard Biggs
Lennier	Bill Mumy
Marcus Cole	Jason Carter
Lyta Alexander	Patricia Tallman
Vir Cotto	Stephen Furst

Guest Stars

Corwin	Joshua Cox
Matthew Duffin	James Warwick
Jacque Lee	Wylie Small
Kat	Kathryn Cressida
Man	Michael McKenzie
Duncan	Aubrey Morris
Dr. Harrison	Carrie Dobro
Lurker	Roger Rook
Trader	Donald Willis
Woman	Leslie Pratt
Vendor	Ross Gottstein

Cheers fill Earhart's as everyone at the bar raises his glass to David Corwin, celebrating his promotion to lieutenant. Corwin, rather embarrassed by all the attention, raises his glass in response. Sheridan knows that his promotion will mean he has more access to station business and asks Ivanova to find out how far he can be trusted.

Dr. Franklin cuts at the organic filaments entwined

*around the spine of a dead man on the autopsy table. He
pulls out a length of something translucent and
wormlike. It wiggles in his tweezers, and he slips it into
a sample jar. While Franklin waits for the computer
analysis to be completed, he is interrupted by Marcus. A
friend of his, Duncan, is missing.*

*Marcus persuades Franklin to break into Duncan's
quarters where they find a hole gouged out of the wall.
They crawl inside and follow a tunnel leading to Down
Below. There, lying on the floor, is a man. The skin on
his back flexes as an alien creature wraps itself around
his spine. Before Franklin can call security, a PPG is
thrust in his face, and he and Marcus are captured by a
gang of lurkers, one of whom is Duncan.*

*Corwin does not know whether to be excited or
terrified when Ivanova invites him to her quarters for a
"talk." She pours him a cup of illicitly cultivated coffee
and asks him what he would do if there was a
contradiction between following orders and doing what
is right for Earth. "I don't think that's a decision I could
make on my own," he replies. "We have to respect the
chain of command or everything falls apart." Ivanova,
embarrassed at having had to ask him, and despondent
at his reply, ushers him out of her quarters. He is not
ready to be taken into their confidence.*

*The lurkers lock up Franklin and Marcus and refuse
to listen to Franklin's offer to help remove the alien
parasites that control them. "We will hurt you if
necessary," Duncan tells them. "We cannot allow you to
interfere."*

*But they look to Franklin for help when one of their
kind is sick and take him to another room. In all the
panic, the guard on Marcus is lessened and he breaks out
of his prison. Grabbing a PPG, Marcus finds Franklin
and fires at the lights, plunging the room into darkness.
The lurkers scatter and Franklin ducks for cover, but he
does not leave. His patient is dying.*

Duncan tries to explain that the patient will have a

*better life if he can survive with the alien creature inside
him. The creatures were bred half a million years ago to
be living records, travelling the galaxy in various hosts,
gathering information to ensure that knowledge survives
into the future. But Marcus cannot believe he is telling
the truth while the creature is inside of him. So it
wriggles free of Duncan's spine. Duncan screams as the
alien withdraws, and he collapses to the floor. "It's true,
Marcus," says Duncan, looking up into his friend's eyes.
"When it was inside me, I saw birds dying on Orion 7. I
saw cities floating in the air . . . I knew everything."*

*Franklin agrees to supervise the future merging of
aliens and humans to stop any further deaths caused by
inadequate hosts. But it is too late for Duncan. The
creature has permanently damaged his neural system,
and he cannot take another one. So he decides to leave
Babylon 5 to search for some of the things he saw when
he was joined and to "be special, one last time."*

"I'm not really happy with the script on that one," admits
writer J. Michael Straczynski. "It was in the midst of
writing that one that we had a small labor action here on the
stage."

This was the same strike that disrupted the filming of
the third episode. "A Day in the Strife," and it meant Joe
Straczynski had to leave his word processor for several days
to help resolve the dispute. "When I begin writing a script,
very often I don't have notes. I don't tend to outline; I do a
couple of notes on a piece of paper and begin writing. I let
the characters surprise me as I go. That works while the
story is white hot in you and you can see it in your head.
Between the start of the episode being written and the com-
pletion of it there was a four- or five-day gap where I didn't
touch it, and by the time I came back to it, I had lost the
fingerprints of the story. Consequently, the first half is pretty
cool, the second half sort of laid there. It's okay; it's not all it
could have been."

"Exogenesis" appears, at first, to be a standard science

fiction plot of alien parasites taking over and controlling human bodies in a sort of retelling of *Invasion of the Body Snatchers*. The opening scenes help to set this up, with a particularly gruesome sequence in which a man screams in pain as a creature burrows deep into his flesh. "It *was* gruesome," agrees director Kevin Cremin. "In fact, in my cut it was quite a bit more gruesome. I think [producer] John Copeland had even come in and said, 'Boy, this makes your skin crawl.' We had to tone it down a little bit, which is fine. Sometimes you get a little hardened by it when you see all the little bits and pieces that go into it. It definitely grabs your attention early on in the show, though."

By the end of the opening titles, the man is dead, and the malevolent nature of the aliens appears unquestionable. Marcus's liaison with the other Rangers, Samuel, deserts his work when he comes under the aliens' influence, and Marcus's friend Duncan also leaves his old life behind to join up with them. They even lock Franklin and Marcus behind bars. Franklin concludes that Samuel, Duncan, and the other lurkers are being controlled by the alien creatures, something that seems to be confirmed by their behavior and his autopsy of the dead man.

But Franklin is misreading the evidence. When the truth is revealed, it shows how he jumped to the wrong conclusions, how the interpretation of every incident was opposite to the real one. The aliens were not invading human bodies; they were joining with them for the benefit of both themselves and their human hosts. Samuel and Duncan left their old lives behind because they believed they had found a better life with the aliens. The lurkers locked up Franklin and Marcus because it was the easiest way to stop them from interfering, and the man who died was a drug addict whose body, they later realized, was not fit enough to sustain the alien organism.

It is the switch from the audience's expectations that makes the story more engaging. Nothing is quite so boring as a predictable plot. Instead, the episode is a journey of discovery that culminates in the revelation that the aliens'

purpose is to preserve knowledge through subsequent gen-
erations of hosts. The actions that seemed threatening at
the beginning are shown to have a noble purpose by the
end. This is not the first time the importance of the preserva-
tion of knowledge has appeared in *Babylon 5*. The Techno-
mages in Season Two's "The Geometry of Shadows" were
retreating from the coming war in order to preserve their
knowledge.

The character of Duncan provides the Human element
in the story that illuminates the central idea. On one level,
the episode is his story. Marcus's concern for him drives the
plot forward and allows the audience to sympathize with
him, when he is joined with the alien creature and, later,
when the creature leaves his body. Duncan was played by
Aubrey Morris, a recognizable face from film and TV. "It
was a wonderful experience working with him," says director Kevin Cremin. "Such a neat gentleman and a bit of film
history, and that was a terrific experience. He's definitely
getting on in years now, and he does put so much into his
acting that you have to be careful not to tire him out too
early. Physically, it's very demanding for him, and it was a
very physically demanding role, too."

While the plot and the guest characters help explore the
idea behind the episode, the unusual pairing of Franklin and
Marcus explores their characters in a new way. Their ordinary lives do not generally intersect with each other, so
when events conspire to bring them together, the result is
surprising. "I often try different combinations of characters,"
says Joe. "When you put two different characters together,
a dynamic comes out that doesn't happen with somebody
else. You put Vir and Lennier together, you have one
dynamic; you put Vir and Na'Toth together, you have a whole
different dynamic. I wanted to see how these two get along
together, what kinds of conversations they might have. Then
I found that I quite liked how they got along together and
have done it a couple more times since then."

"It's an interesting combination," says Franklin actor
Richard Biggs. "I love working with Jason. I think Jason and

I can really play off each other quite well, and the day seems to go by faster when Jason and I are hanging out. We both have this dry sense of humor. We just click."

"We're obviously contrasting physical types," adds Jason Carter. "I'm the emaciated, European romantic who looks like he's dying of tuberculosis, and he's the power gym hunk that all the models go for! They work because they are from such contrasting perspectives. We thought it was a bit of a buddy picture. I loved the whole scene in the jail. All I'm asking about is Ivanova, and he [Franklin] cannot understand how, facing imminent death in this situation, I could be asking questions about a member of the crew. My reply is, 'Can you think of a better time?', [the idea being] if you've got some questions to ask, you better ask them now."

The lively banter between Franklin and Marcus clearly brings a lot of fun to the episode, which is also reflected in the subplot involving Ivanova and Lieutenant Corwin. Corwin, played by Joshua Cox, began in the background as one of the techs operating in C&C, then gradually, over a series of episodes, began to emerge into the foreground. "I like to take credit partially for keeping his job and actually getting him a name," says Claudia Christian, who plays Ivanova. "He started as a tech, and I just kept telling everybody how responsible and professional and good he was, and then I said, 'Hey, why don't you give him a name?' Then he became Corwin, and then Lieutenant Corwin, and pretty soon he had a part every so often. It's nice because he is sweet and a good kid, so you might as well reward excellence."

The comedy comes from the subtext that runs through the episode. While the audience knows exactly why Ivanova and Corwin act the way they do, they continue to keep it a secret from each other. "I love comedies of error," says Joe. "It just tickled me that she might make this first invitation, but she might be misconstrued as asking him on a date, or close to it, and see him greet this with a mix of enthusiasm and terror, knowing that Ivanova is the person involved here, which is certainly how I would react."

Corwin buys Ivanova a bunch of synthetic roses, then

thinks better of telling her he bought them, only to discover they were a present she would have enjoyed. In the final comedy of error, Ivanova concludes they must have come from Marcus and gives them back to him. But all that does is encourage Marcus to pursue their relationship, which he continues to do for the rest of the season.

8
"Messages from Earth"

Cast

Captain John Sheridan	Bruce Boxleitner
Commander Susan Ivanova	Claudia Christian
Security Chief Michael Garibaldi	Jerry Doyle
Ambassador Delenn	Mira Furlan
Citizen G'Kar	Andreas Katsulas
Ambassador Londo Mollari	Peter Jurasik
Dr. Stephen Franklin	Richard Biggs
Lennier	Bill Mumy
Marcus Cole	Jason Carter
Lyta Alexander	Patricia Tallman
Vir Cotto	Stephen Furst

Guest Stars

Cook	Loraine Shields
Dr. Mary Kirkish	Nancy Stafford
Security Guard No. 1	Vaughn Armstrong
Security Guard No. 2	Merrin Dungey

Marcus lashes out with his Minbari fighting pike, striking one man in the face and another in the stomach, and then runs after Dr. Mary Kirkish. He finds her unconscious on the floor with a third man ready to shoot her through the head. With a yell, Marcus knocks him to the floor and punches him out cold. He turns to the woman and checks that she is still alive.

The men were sent to kill Dr. Kirkish because of what she knows and what she might tell others. She was working for Interplanetary Expeditions when she was sent to Ganymede on an archaeological dig and found a Shadow vessel. She went on the run when she discovered what Earth was planning to do with it, hoping to bring the information to others. She tells Sheridan that Earth plans to excavate the ship, examine it, and eventually, use it against other races, and possibly even Humans. Sheridan decides the only way to stop that from happening is to use the White Star.

Sheridan tries to get some sleep on the Minbari ship as it makes its long journey toward Earth's solar system. Delenn listens with a smile as he talks about home, his father, and the sound of rain on a roof. "Right now, more than anything else in the world, I wish it would rain," he says. Delenn speaks some Minbari words, and the ship responds with the sound that Sheridan longs to hear. Delenn holds his hand as he lies back on the bed and, at last, drifts off to sleep to the sound of raindrops.

A jump point opens and the White Star *enters normal space and is dwarfed by the mass of Jupiter behind it. They tap into the audio signals from Ganymede as a volunteer is guided into the Shadow ship to merge with it. "Oh my God. It's moving!" cries a voice as the ship begins to wake. It flies erratically into space, shooting energy beams in all directions. The* White Star *fires at it, but the Shadow ship is hardly damaged. "If we can't outfight it, let's hope we can outthink it," says Sheridan, and he orders the* White Star *to head into the mass of Jupiter.*

The White Star *plunges into the Jovian atmosphere, with the Shadow ship following. The crew begins to lose control as the hull of the* White Star *buckles under Jupiter's ever-increasing gravity. Sheridan urges them on until the last moment, then the* White Star *turns, struggling against the pull of the planet, and uses all its energy to escape. The Shadow ship flies past them and realizes—too late—what is going on. It tries to turn, but Jupiter is too strong and the vessel is crushed like a dried leaf.*

The White Star *pulls away from Jupiter to find the Earth Alliance destroyer* Agamemnon *waiting for it.*

Sheridan freezes, unable to fire on his old ship or suggest any other course of action. Delenn takes the initiative and calls for the jump engines to be put on line. Sheridan follows her lead and orders a jump point to be formed within the Jovian atmosphere. The jump point opens, crackling with energy as it ignites the surrounding hydrogen. But it is stable enough for the White Star to enter and head for home.

Nightwatch knows Sheridan forged station logs to cover his four-day absence and asks Zack to get Garibaldi to tell him what is going on. Zack is reluctant to betray a friend, but Nightwatch tells him he has a choice to make between betraying a friendship and protecting Earth.

"Messages from Earth," "Point of No Return," and "Severed Dreams" are three linked episodes that bring *Babylon 5* to a crisis point. For a long time, the command staff has been working behind the scenes to uncover the conspirators on Earth and build an alliance to fight the Shadows. But as matters accelerate, behind-the-scenes work is not enough, and Sheridan and the others have to face their own government if they are to finish what they have started.

Unusually, the episode makes reference to events outlined in a series of comic books written during the second season and based on story notes by J. Michael Straczynski. In issues five to eight, Garibaldi relates the story of his first meeting with Jeffrey Sinclair (Season One's commander), when they saw a Shadow ship being excavated on Mars. Dr. Mary Kirkish retells this story from an archaeologist's point of view before revealing that another Shadow vessel has been found on Ganymede. (Garibaldi told an abbreviated version of this story in "Infection.")

It sets in motion events that bring Babylon 5 into direct conflict with Earth, raising the tension and putting everything at stake for the characters. "There's a moment when you're driving along and you hit an open stretch of road, and you can rev the engine and go as fast as you can, which is what I did with writing these three episodes," says Joe Straczynski. "Just floor it and try and hold on to it as you go without flipping over. This one was where I thought I'm going to really show what we can do with the show and take all the things we had started to lay in—the Nightwatch, the Mars situation, the Shadows, and all of this stuff—and drag it screaming out into the light."

The tension builds as Sheridan takes the *White Star* to Earth's solar system. The enormity of the risk he is taking is underlined by the instructions he leaves with the others in case he does not return. But as the *White Star* heads for certain conflict at Ganymede, the episode takes a breather and gives us a tender scene between Sheridan and Delenn. He recollects how his father helped him fall asleep by using the garden hose to simulate rain falling on the roof, and Delenn responds by reproducing the sound inside the *White Star*. It is a very simple moment between these two, and it works on several levels.

"It's a chance to set up Sheridan's father in more detail, since Kosh will be taking advantage of that very soon," says Joe Straczynski. "It further tightens the Sheridan/Delenn relationship, and it's a very fragile moment for him. This is a character who, for the good of everyone, has to maintain a certain discipline and a certain rock-solidness about his own personality, and he's going in against the government and he has a very vulnerable moment. You see he really is afraid of doing this; he really is uncomfortable and nervous."

"It's a very loving speech," adds Sheridan actor Bruce Boxleitner. "I think he has a lot of respect for his father. His father did these things for him, and he knew it, and I think those kinds of things are good. I don't think they're overly sentimental. I think it's good to know those sides of people. We shouldn't be afraid, sometimes, of sentiment in these cynical times we live in. People exist in their hearts. It's also building this relationship, endearing them to each other, finding out about each other."

By this time, Sheridan and Delenn's relationship is clearly on a strong foundation, but it is still a subtle thing. Their actions and their body language say it all, even though they are not ready to admit it verbally. It is that slow, gentle, teasing progression, which Mira Furlan, who plays Delenn, found surprising. "I think it's done in a masterly way; I don't know how he does it," she says. "I know that fans are eager to see 'When are you going to kiss? When is the kiss going to happen?' So he [Joe Straczynski] knows how to build that suspense between us, and he never gives us too much. I remember with that scene where we go to dinner [in "A Race Through Dark Places"], I thought, Why doesn't she come to his bedroom? I wanted to somehow have a continuation then in that episode, but it was not time because Joe has this arc in his head and just doesn't allow things to go more quickly than this huge thing requires."

Showing Sheridan's Human frailties before he goes into battle invites the audience to care about him. He may be a stoic military leader on the bridge of the *White Star*, but it is the man behind the soldier that the audience is rooting for. "He writes Sheridan in that he's got a great tactical mind," says Bruce. "He [Sheridan] may fall down in a few other things, but he knows how to work with the least and make the most out of an opportunity. He has this thing—the military man—he cannot compete with the Shadows in firepower, [so he thinks], 'Maybe we can outmaneuver them, use your enemy's strength against himself.' That's a very martial arts thing, forcing the enemy to use his own brutal force against himself. That's what we do with the Shadows continuously."

The special effects in a battle scene like this play a large part in conveying the action, and Foundation Imaging produced some stunning shots of the *White Star* and the Shadow vessel plunging toward Jupiter. But what is important to the story is the fate of the people inside the ship. Mike Vejar was the director on this episode, and his job was to help bring out the Human drama of the situation. "As for the visual effects done on that show, you can't, when you're directing it, hope that they're going to pull you out," he says. "You have to try and build as much tension as you can within the scenes themselves. That, again, involves a lot of cutting. So I have to get a lot of coverage [variety of shots] and get the actors to a point where they believe they are in a firefight or in a battle. Not just moving from position to position, but actually give them that sense of professional tension. They're all military, so they can't be over the top, but getting that sense that something is dangerous and happening at the moment. You hope that the visual effects will pull you out, but you don't necessarily depend on them."

Mike Vejar likes to build the tension by allowing the actors to play the whole sequence through, rather than chopping it into its component parts. "I think that helps a lot," he says. "Also, building a sense of the pace that you want to see [with the actors on set]. Making it real tight and quick so there aren't long pauses or descriptions, where I'm saying, 'The ship is blowing up and all this stuff is happening,' but actually giving them very succinct, short cues and keeping the thing moving so you can see their tension building as the scene does."

The *White Star*, of course, triumphs and returns safely to Babylon 5 for an apparently happy ending. But the characters are not to be let off that easily. Nightwatch is strengthening its presence on the station, and Zack is put under pressure to find out information from Garibaldi. Zack refuses at first, but by the end of the scene, the audience is not sure if he will join up with the "bad guys" or not. Jeff Conaway always sees his character as a good guy, and that's the way he wanted to portray him, even when it was uncertain which way he would turn. "It's kind of interesting to watch somebody with good intentions going the wrong way," he says. "They don't even know that's what's happening; they're just naturally doing that. Fan letters and when I've been out at conventions, people say, 'Oh man, I really thought you were going down the wrong road, and I thought you were a bad guy. I liked you, but I couldn't understand why you were doing these things.' Then I was successful because you want the audience to like you no matter what."

The problems with Nightwatch are a reminder that the fight is not over yet. In the last scene, martial law is declared on Earth and the crisis steps up another notch.

9
"Point of No Return"

Cast

Captain John Sheridan ....Bruce Boxleitner
Commander Susan Ivanova ....Claudia Christian
Security Chief Michael Garibaldi ....Jerry Doyle
Ambassador Delenn ....Mira Furlan
Citizen G'Kar ....Andreas Katsulas
Ambassador Londo Mollari ....Peter Jurasik
Dr. Stephen Franklin ....Richard Biggs
Lennier ....Bill Mumy
Marcus Cole ....Jason Carter
Lyta Alexander ....Patricia Tallman
Vir Cotto ....Stephen Furst

Guest Stars

Centauri Official ....Milton James
Passing Minbari ....Jonathan Chapman
ISN Newscaster...Maggie Egan
Lt. General O'Reilly ....Ed Trotta
Corwin ....Joshua Cox
Security Guard ....Vaughn Armstrong
Lady Morella ....Majel Barrett
General Smits.......................................Lewis Arquette
Ta'Lon ....Marshall Teague
Man ....Tony Rayner
Nightwatch Guard ....Gunther Jensen

Following the declaration of martial law on Earth, General Smits tells Sheridan that responsibility for all off-world security has been given to Nightwatch. Sheridan starts to object, but Smits cuts him short. "Our job is to follow orders from the commander in chief and respect the chain of command," he says. "I suggest you try to see this as an opportunity, not a burden."

Garibaldi storms into the squad room, where Zack

and the others in Nightwatch are in the process of converting his security team. He grabs a table with both hands and tips it over, scattering paperwork and armbands on the floor. "If anything I've ever said or done has meant a damn to you, stop this." He looks around the room, searching each of their faces, but they all avoid his gaze. Nightwatch relieves him of duty, and Zack is put in charge.

Londo has invited Lady Morella, prophetess and wife of the late Centauri emperor Turhan, to Babylon 5. Londo arranged the visit on the pretext of showing her the station, but in truth, he wants her to "see" for him. "I believe . . . I am meant for something greater," he tells her. "A greater darkness or a greater good, I can no longer say."

Sheridan's face appears on monitors across the station, declaring martial law. Back in his office, he takes a last look at his orders from Earth before crumpling them up and throwing them across the room. Then he remembers something General Smits said, and his despondency is replaced by a glimmer of hope: "Respect the chain of command . . ."

Zack opens the door to his quarters and stops when he sees that Garibaldi, Ivanova, and G'Kar are waiting for him. Sheridan approaches from behind, and Zack has no choice but to step inside. Later, Zack tells another Nightwatch security guard about his meeting with the captain. "They wanted me to help them," he confesses, "but I can't."

G'Kar, inspired by his recent religious experience, has enlisted the other Narns on the station to become security personnel, replacing the Nightwatch security guards. In return, he tells Sheridan, "I want 'in.' "

Nightwatch security guards arm themselves and crowd into the docking bay, ready to overpower the Narns that are being brought in to replace them. Zack discreetly toggles his link. "Now!" he says, and dives out of the docking bay just as the doors close, trapping the

Delenn shows Sheridan on board the White Star *in 'Matters of Honor'*

'Voices of Authority':
Ivanova enters the Great
Machine of Epsilon 3

'Dust to Dust': Londo and Vir recover after G'Kar's attack

Ivanova gets acquainted with the controls of the White Star

Delenn tries to persuade G'Kar to attend a Minbari rebirth ceremony in 'Ceremonies of Light and Dark'

Sheridan catches Delenn as she is stabbed in 'Ceremonies of Light and Dark'

*Vir and his new
found love,
Lyndisty, in 'Sic
Transit Vir'*

*Michael York
believes he is
King Arthur in
'A Late Delivery
from Avalon'*

'Ship of Tears': Carolyn, one of the
telepaths altered by the Shadows, connects
her brain to the systems in Medlab

Sheridan takes the helm of the White Star in 'War Without End'

'War Without End': Sinclair prepares to change into Valen

Sinclair and Delenn face the future and the past in 'War Without End'

Lyta Alexander bleeds from her eye as she makes telepathic contact with a Shadow vessel in 'Walkabout'

'Grey 17 is Missing':
Garibaldi and
Jeremiah are about
to face The Zarg

'Z'ha'dum': Sheridan is
reunited with Anna, the
wife he thought was dead

Nightwatch guards inside. Sheridan places them all under arrest for conspiracy to mutiny and failure to obey the chain of command. The Nightwatch had been ordered to take control by the political office, which, he reminds them, has no jurisdiction over military personnel. Garibaldi congratulates Zack for doing the right thing. "Yeah," says Zack, pleased with himself. "This time, maybe I did."

Lady Morella tells Londo that he still has three opportunities to avoid the fire that awaits him. "You must save the eye that does not see," she says. "You must not kill the one who is already dead. And, at the last, you must surrender yourself to your greatest fear, knowing that it will destroy you." She adds that becoming emperor is a part of his destiny that he cannot avoid, and that Vir will also become emperor. Vir begins to laugh, but it is no joke. "One of you will become emperor after the other is dead."

Ivanova approaches Sheridan in his office and tells him that four out of the five ships that were fighting Earth under the command of General Hague have been shot down. "They'll be coming for us next," Sheridan replies.

The role of Lady Morella was specially written for Majel Barrett, the wife of the late *Star Trek* creator Gene Roddenberry. "We heard that she was nice-mouthing the show at various places, speaking very well of it," says Joe. "She felt that the feud between a certain party of *Trek* fans and *B5* fans was pointless and silly, and she wanted to put her money where her mouth was, as it were, and come on the show and say, 'If I can do this, why can't you at least watch the show?' It was a very nice gesture to make and got us a fair amount of publicity and made some *Trek* fans give us a second chance. I wrote the part for her, obliquely referring to Gene Roddenberry and her relationship to him, although I tried not to go too deep into the well for that one."

"I can honestly say that she carried around a great burden

being a Roddenberry in life," says Peter Jurasik, who plays Londo. "When she enters a group of science fiction fans or comes onto our set—a science fiction community—the waters just part for her and people just kind of stand back. That's one of the things she needed to overcome as an actress in order to get to the work, and I really respect that . . . It sounds like I'm making excuses for her, but she certainly doesn't need me to do that; the performance stands on its own. Whenever you have to be prophetic, it's like playing blind or drunk; it's a pitfall that can very easily trip you up, and I thought she did a really nice job of it."

Lady Morella's prophecy foreshadows Londo's future in a way he does not understand. This technique is something Joe Straczynski has continued to build into the fabric of *Babylon 5*, setting out markers for the storyline that, in the main, he has to keep to. "I like to create challenges for myself," he says. "If someone knows the ending of a story, then the natural reaction is, 'Well, nothing can happen now of interest to me.' My feeling is, 'I'll tell you the ending because I want to make the road there very interesting, and you're never going to know how I'm going to get there.' So it was a nice thing to play with the audience that way."

Her revelation that Vir and Londo will each become emperor came as a surprise to Vir, but was it a surprise to the actor? "A little bit, but I have an idea of what's going on," says Stephen Furst. "The fans love it. I do science fiction conventions, and they all want to know when I'll be emperor."

"Isn't that a great twist?" adds Peter Jurasik. "A wonderful piece of writing by Joe. What can be more disturbing to Londo and Vir at that moment than them both getting the prediction in front of each other. Then, of course, he pays it off with this great Laurel and Hardy scene, when they're both stuck at either ends of the couch. That was terrific to play, by the way. The director just stuck us at opposite ends of the couch and said 'Do whatever you want, relax and have a good time.' I kind of felt, and Stephen did, too, that we could have done that scene for hours. It's the kind of stuff where you tap into an energy and think, 'Gee, I'd love to do a two-hour comedy movie with this person,' because Stephen and I really have a good old time together when we get on the set."

Londo's and Vir's personal revelations continue against the background of heightened crisis for the Humans. Babylon 5 has never been an isolated space station, and one of the things the episode does is emphasize how events back on Earth have a direct bearing on the Earth-run station. ISN reports are laced through the episode, and the characters watch helplessly as events that will shape their future occur many light-years away, out of their control. The major event is General Hague's attempt to launch a counterstrike against President Clark, and his subsequent fight with Earth Alliance forces, but Joe Straczynski felt it important to concentrate on the characters' reactions to these events rather than the space battle. "The battle that we see taking place on the monitors, we see from a distance, over someone's shoulder; we never really get a good look at it. Oddly enough, that works to make it more real, because you're used to seeing news coming over televisions on newscasts."

Babylon 5, meanwhile, finds itself outmaneuvered as Nightwatch takes over security and control slips away from Sheridan and his command staff. Garibaldi's instant reaction is to confront them head-on, despite Sheridan's warning that he should stop and think of a better way to solve the problem. It's a personal snub for him, and one he feels he must confront. "I got to flip the tables over and the furniture and stuff like that, which is great," says actor Jerry Doyle. "It's the stuff you'd like to do at home, but you can't. But here you can, and someone resets it for you and says, 'That was great, smash some more stuff.' It was a fun scene to play because you get a chance to smash up the scenery. It was written well and shot in a [no-edit] master on a hand-held steadicam."

Nothing is so straightforward for Sheridan. He tells Garibaldi that he will find a solution to their predicament, but in truth, at the beginning of the episode, he has nowhere to turn. The conflict he faces between following orders and doing what he feels is right is just as much an internal conflict as it is an external one. "Everything he has learned is now being turned upside down," explains Bruce Boxleitner. "Everything that he trusted and relied upon. EarthForce was his life, his duty, his honor. All of that is being turned upside down. [He's thinking,] 'What do I do now? What is the right thing to do?' It is a point of no return, and he has to take a step forward into the decision he made."

The solution involves enlisting Zack's help to trap the Nightwatch. Zack was always treading a fine line up until this point, siding with Nightwatch because it was easier to play along, while becoming increasingly uncomfortable with what they were asking him to do. In "Point of No Return," he is forced to make a choice between Nightwatch and loyalty to Babylon 5. The audience is kept guessing which way he will fall right up until the last minute. "It all comes to a head there," says actor Jeff Conaway. "It's funny, because I was talking to John Copeland one week, and he said, 'Oh, in this episode coming up, you're going to be the hero,' and I said, 'Well, I thought I was a hero!' and he said, 'Well, with Joe you never know quite what he is going to do.' "

The episode pulls off the denouement by showing the audience selective information. We don't see the scene in which Sheridan and the others persuade Zack to help them, making it seem, at first, as if he has betrayed them. Earlier in the episode, General Smits gives Sheridan clues, when he tells him to "respect the chain of command" and use it as an "opportunity" to solve the Nightwatch problem. Such skillful plotting is just a little bit too neat for Joe Straczynski. "It's almost a little bit too clever for its own good in the resolution of the Nightwatch story. It's almost a little too clever and facile, and I have to be careful of that.

"There's a sense of a great doom and foreshadowing about that episode," Joe continues. "Some episodes, more than others, are mood pieces, and 'Point of No Return' definitely qualifies as a mood piece." It ends, similarly to "Messages from Earth," with what seems to be a happy ending. But it is not a happy ending at all, just a minor victory in a much bigger battle. Sheridan acknowledges to Ivanova that Earth forces will be coming for them next, and the mood is set for the final showdown.

10
"Severed Dreams"

Cast

Captain John Sheridan	Bruce Boxleitner
Commander Susan Ivanova	Claudia Christian
Security Chief Michael Garibaldi	Jerry Doyle
Ambassador Delenn	Mira Furlan
Citizen G'Kar	Andreas Katsulas
Ambassador Londo Mollari	Peter Jurasik
Dr. Stephen Franklin	Richard Biggs
Lennier	Bill Mumy
Marcus Cole	Jason Carter
Lyta Alexander	Patricia Tallman
Vir Cotto	Stephen Furst

Guest Stars

Narn	Kim Strauss
Major Ed Ryan	Bruce McGill
Lieutenant Bill Trainor	Phil Morris
Drakhen	James Parks
ISN Reporter No. 1	Maggie Egan
Corwin	Joshua Cox
Capt. Sandra Hiroshi	Kim Miyori
ISN Reporter No. 2	Matt Gottlieb
Religious Minbari	Jonathan Chapman
David Sheridan	Rance Howard

General Hague is dead, killed during a firefight with Earth forces. His ship, the Alexander, *arrives at Babylon 5, under the command of Major Ryan, for a rest and a chance to make repairs. But President Clark knows where they are and has sent a fleet to seize control of the station.*

Earth forces are bombing Mars because they refused to accept martial law. As an ISN newscaster relays the information, another reporter interrupts with

*information Clark does not want released. The Orion 7
and Proxima 3 colonies have broken away from Earth in
protest over the Mars action. The reporter flinches as he
hears gunfire in the background. "There's information
you don't have," he continues earnestly. "What's been
going on for the last year, we haven't been allowed to tell
you, we . . ." There's an explosion in the ISN studio; the
place descends into panic, and the picture abruptly turns
to static.*

*Delenn faces the ruling Minbari Grey Council for the
first time since she was expelled. Wars have erupted
between other races, and the Humans are fighting
among themselves; the Grey Council has decided not to
get involved. "We must stand with the others now
before it is too late," she tells them. "Break the Council
and come with me."*

*Sheridan's holographic image appears throughout the
station. "As of this moment, Babylon 5 is seceding from
the Earth Alliance," he announces to the shocked
crowds. "We will remain an independent state until
President Clark is removed from office." Sheridan's
image disappears, and he sighs to himself, realizing what
he has just done.*

*The jumpgate opens and an EarthForce assault fleet
enters Babylon 5 space. Enemy fighters lock on and
strike at Babylon 5 and its Starfuries with streams of
energy pulses. The* Alexander *responds, intercepting the
pulses and striking at the Earth cruisers with a
penetrating energy beam.*

*A breaching pod attaches itself to the station's hull. It
blows a hole in the wall, and soldiers scramble inside,
guns ready. Garibaldi's Human and Narn security forces
advance on them, and the air is filled with crisscrossing
PPG blasts. One Narn is hit in the chest and falls to the
ground. Then another. And another.*

*Three enemy Starfuries head straight for Babylon 5.
Pulse cannons respond, and two of the Starfuries break
off to avoid the onslaught. The third is hit and is sent
careening toward the station. It strikes the blast doors of*

the Observation Dome with an explosion that shoots sparks across the deck and knocks Sheridan to the floor.

Babylon 5's defense grid throws everything it has at the assault force's lead ship. Sheridan offers a chance for it to surrender, but it is too late, myriad explosions erupt within it and it floats away from the station, dead. Lieutenant Corwin looks relieved. "Good thing this stopped when it did, we couldn't take much more . . ." His words trail off as the jumpgate fires open, and a flood of EarthForce destroyers emerges, demanding Babylon 5's surrender. Sheridan's face clouds over.

Four more jump points form outside, and just as Sheridan is overcome with hopelessness, he sees the most welcome face imaginable. "This is Ambassador Delenn of the Minbari," she says from the head of an impressive Minbari fleet. "Babylon 5 is under our protection. Withdraw or be destroyed." Faced with such unbeatable odds, the Earth ships turn tail and retreat into hyperspace.

Many lay dead or dying after the attack, but the station has survived, and as Sheridan walks into the Zocalo he is greeted by a crowd of people who break into spontaneous applause.

"Severed Dreams" brings to a close the trilogy of episodes in which Babylon 5 is forced to make a stand against Earth. It was the climax to the story line and the toughest one for Joe Straczynski to write. "Because the emotional stakes are so high," he says, "the only way you can write convincingly about a character having a certain emotion is to put yourself in that place and feel those emotions yourself. The writer's job is to touch passion, be burned by it, and come back and tell you what it was like; I had to go through what the characters went through. It was also paying off so much that had been set up, and there's always the terror of 'Oh my God, what if I can't pull this off?' I know what I want to do, but there's often light-years between what I want to do and what I end up doing. Every artist, I think, feels that. And oddly enough, it was a very quick write, too. It was difficult, and it was quick. I think I wrote the whole script in two or three days. So it was emotionally grinding but very satisfying at the end. I didn't want to write it until I was absolutely ready to tell the whole thing and told everyone, 'Don't bother me.' Everyone knew. 'Don't bother Joe, this is an important one.' I got through it very quickly, while it was still hot in my brain, and it came out very well."

After "The Fall of Night," "Severed Dreams" was the show's most intense episode in terms of special effects. Extra people were brought in to complete the CGI shots on time, and even then they were delivered at the last minute. But while this fantastic lightshow was raging outside the station, a much grittier battle was raging inside as security teams fought hand-to-hand with invading marines. "It was absolutely important to me to show the hand-to-hand combat Down Below," says Joe. "When ships are being destroyed, when the bad guys get hit, we're used to cheering for that. It's a little harder when you see the face of the enemy, seeing them get a gun butt to the face or being shot down."

It was during these hand-to-hand combat scenes that Jerry Doyle broke his arm. He had a fight sequence in which Garibaldi was supposed to hit a marine in the chest, another in the head, another with the butt of his gun, and then run on. But one of the stuntmen fell on the floor in the wrong place, so when Jerry turned to run, he tripped over him. "My legs went out, and I came down and snapped my elbow on the ground," he says. "I knew something was wrong, and I'm laying there just sweating, going, 'Goddamn, this hurts.' Then the director said, 'We've got kind of a problem, we kinda missed it.' I'm like, 'What do you mean you've missed it?' He goes, 'We didn't get it on B camera . . . We need to do it again,' and I go, 'Well, there's something definitely wrong with my arm here. I'm not sure if I'm going to throw up, shit in my pants, pass out, or all of the above.' I said, 'If you want to shoot this fucking scene again, get the camera set, get everybody back in fucking place, and do it now!' He's like [timid] 'Okay, let's . . .' So we did the thing again, and I'll be goddamned, the same thing happened again! I went down again, and that's when it got my wrist."

"He was in excruciating pain, and he still had another scene to shoot," remembers director David Eagle. "We wanted to whisk him off to the hospital, but he insisted on staying to finish that scene."

It was the final part of the sequence, when Garibaldi, tired and wounded from the battle, is helped by Zack to rest against the wall. "My arm was pretty dead, and I was in that pre-shocky kind of thing," says Jerry. "I had to hit my mark and drop all my shit and slide down to the floor, and the director looks at me and says, 'And do it with that *exact* look on your face.' Then we did it. They cut the clothes off, threw some clothes on me, and I went off to the hospital."

There were more behind-the-scenes troubles with General Hague, played in earlier episodes by Robert Foxworth. The Major Ryan part in "Severed Dreams" was originally written for him, but he was double booked by his agent and ended up working on a *Star Trek: Deep Space Nine* episode instead. "Suddenly we had to adapt," remembers Bruce Boxleitner. "I'd had this relationship with him; I was working for him espionage-wise, and now he's dead! So Bruce McGill came in and played Major So-and-so [Ryan], and this is where we had the famous outtake." Sheridan asks Ryan, 'Where's General Hague?' and Ryan looks back with a troubled face and replies, 'He's on *Deep Space Nine!*' "

In the midst of all the space battles and action are people. The episode constantly puts the characters in danger, increasing the ante. Ivanova takes a Starfury and joins the other pilots on the front line. Before she goes, there is a silent moment between her and Sheridan that conveys that danger and how much they care for each other, more than words could say.

But perhaps the most poignant moment is between Sheridan and his father (Rance Howard), when he calls home for what could be the last time. "Those things get me; those scenes really get me," says Bruce Boxleitner. "All the guys on the set—it was very interesting—they're all doing their thing, lighting and everything, and we're rehearsing, and Rance went, 'Son,' and every guy kind of [stopped and looked]. He's like everybody's dad; he just has that sort of lovable quality about him."

The key moment for Delenn is her return to the Grey Council. She has to face them for the first time since she was thrown out for following Valen's prophecy. Her purpose is to persuade them that they must return to the path of prophecy, break the Council, and follow her. That moment is punctuated when Delenn takes a staff from one of the Grey Council members and breaks it in two. The scene went smoothly for Mira Furlan until she had to break the staff. "The problem was incredible, and it frustrated me unbelievably," she says, "I always broke it in a different place. I couldn't know in advance where exactly it was going to break and how strong I had to press in order to break it. It kept being different. First, it was too easy to break. It was this climax, and when it came to that bit, it was so anticlimactic. You wanted this huge break, you wanted the accent to the scene after your huge monologue, but no, it came out like you broke a toothpick! Then they tried to make it so it was very hard to break, and then I couldn't break it. It's just those little things that go completely out of control."

Delenn's scene with the Grey Council sets up the moment at the end when she leads the Minbari fleet to save the station. Babylon 5 is at its most desperate point when, metaphorically, the seventh cavalry comes over the hill. It is enough to scare the Earth forces into retreat, and victory is secured. But as the camera pans around Brown Sector, where the forces were in hand-to-hand combat, it shows that the victory was not without cost. "I hate leaving an audience feeling cocky about an episode and 'how wonderful for us,' " says Joe Straczynski. "Most shows would have faded out after Sheridan said, 'All ships return to base. The crisis is over now.' It was important to show the cost of that victory in bodies, and people in pain, and Garibaldi being hurt. Victory or battle is not something to be cheered; you're thankful that you made it through alive. Jingoism is not the style of the show, and it was important to conclude with what most shows wouldn't have shown."

11
"Ceremonies of Light and Dark"

Cast

Captain John Sheridan ....Bruce Boxleitner
Commander Susan Ivanova ....Claudia Christian
Security Chief Michael Garibaldi ....Jerry Doyle
Ambassador Delenn ....Mira Furlan
Citizen G'Kar ....Andreas Katsulas
Ambassador Londo Mollari ....Peter Jurasik
Dr. Stephen Franklin ....Richard Biggs
Lennier ....Bill Mumy
Marcus Cole ....Jason Carter
Lyta Alexander ....Patricia Tallman
Vir Cotto ....Stephen Furst

Guest Stars

Boggs ....Don Stroud
The Sniper ....Paul Perri
Corwin ....Joshua Cox
Refa ....William Forward
Lenann ....Kim Strauss
Morden ....Ed Wasser
Thug No. 1......................................Jim Cody Williams
Guard ....Doug McCoy
Maintenance Man ....Vincent Bilancio

The senior officers stand to attention to honor those who died defending Babylon 5. Ivanova recites their names, "Hamilton . . . Rodriguez . . . Spinelli . . . Singh . . . Osterman . . ." as a stream of coffins exits the docking bay and sails into the sun.

Lord Refa looks aghast at his empty glass as Londo tells him his drink was poisoned. It is a poison that comes in two halves. In order to escape ingesting the second deadly half, Londo tells Refa that he must pull the Centauri troops back from minor conflicts, strengthen defenses around Centauri Prime, and have nothing more to do with Mr. Morden.

Delenn plans to hold a Minbari ceremony in which everyone will be asked to leave their pain behind them in order to be "reborn." Each person must tell someone a secret they have never told anyone before and give up something of great personal value. Marcus protests that he has nothing to give up; he lost everything when the Shadows attacked his home. "Then that is exactly what you must give up," says Delenn. "You have let go of the people, the places, the things, but you have not let go of the pain."

Delenn enters the docking bay to greet one of the captains from the Minbari fleet that is protecting Babylon 5. But her smile turns to confusion as the doors slam shut behind her and men appear with PPGs to take them captive.

Boggs, the leader of the kidnappers, tells Sheridan over the monitor, "Either you get rid of those Minbari cruisers in the next six hours, or we'll kill them." Boggs scrambled the signal so it could not be traced, but the background hum of a coolant system gives Sheridan a clue.

Marcus beats up every single person in the Down Below bar, desperate for information about Delenn. Lennier, however, wants to talk about the rebirth ceremony. It was the last thing Delenn asked him to do, and he intends to see that it is done. As part of the ceremony, he tells Marcus something about Delenn he has never told anyone before. "I love her," he says. "It is not romantic love as you consider it. It is something higher and nobler."

Security teams rush the kidnappers. PPG blasts fly across the room as Delenn and the Minbari captain run for safety. One of the kidnappers raises a knife toward

Sheridan. "John!" screams Delenn. She runs toward him as the man throws the blade. It strikes Delenn in the back, and she collapses in Sheridan's arms. Sheridan chases after the man, grabs him, and, with a punch born of anger, knocks him to the ground.

Delenn lies in Medlab, unable to conduct the rebirth ceremony. So the rebirth ceremony comes to her. Sheridan enters holding his EarthForce uniform. He lays it to the side as a symbol of giving up what it once stood for. Then he tells her a secret he has never told anyone before. "I realized I've never told you how much I care for you."

The others follow, each giving up their uniforms and each revealing their secrets. Garibaldi: "I'm afraid, all of the time, of what I might do if I ever let go." Ivanova: "I think I loved Talia." Franklin: "I think I have a problem."

In return, Delenn has had something made for them, and later, all five enter the Observation Dome wearing new uniforms. "The crisis, for now, is over," says Sheridan. "Tell the ships, we're open for business."

"Ceremonies of Light and Dark" immediately follows Babylon 5's break away from Earth and marks a deliberate change of pace. Joe Straczynski calls it a "shake-down period," a chance for the audience and the characters to adjust to the new situation. "People aren't used to major upheavals in the structure of their television shows," he says. "If you look at the first episode of a series and the last episode of a series, there isn't usually that much difference between the two. We have major changes, and anyone who has ever driven a stick-shift car knows that if you try and jam it too fast into gear, it's going to grind. So we had to have some moments when you pop the clutch and move it into the next gear, and episodes like this one help to do that."

It is a coming to terms for the characters, a time for them to take stock of the past and prepare for the future. Londo continues to manipulate his own destiny and that of Centauri Prime. Having distanced himself from Morden and his Shadow associates, he proceeds to ensure that Refa (William Forward) does the same. "We had a great time that day," says Peter Jurasik, who plays Londo. "It was a very talky, long scene that could have been burdensome and tiresome to do, but instead, we could have done it over and over again because we both enjoyed interacting as those two characters. It's part of the advantage of the repertory of characters. Bill coming back and Londo and Refa developing a relationship, but also Bill Forward and Peter Jurasik developing a relationship."

Londo's attempt to manipulate the future echoes the theme of the episode as a whole—leaving the pain behind and preparing to face the future. This is, of course, the purpose of Delenn's rebirth ceremony. Not everyone wants to take part, however. Londo is dealing with his future in his own way, while G'Kar has already turned to a new direction following his religious experience. Surprisingly, Marcus, a product of Minbari training, is also reluctant, feeling he cannot do what the ceremony asks of him "That's an interesting philosophical debate that comes up: I like that one," says actor Jason Carter. "He didn't have anything left to give up because he's lost everything, his friends and his family, and Delenn is saying the thing you have to give up is that, that guilt that you're still alive and that preoccupation. It's like anybody who gives up something. If someone gives up smoking, and then becomes a born-again nonsmoker, campaigning against smoking all over the world because they're so convinced smoking is bad, it is replacing an addiction with another addiction. It's not a detachment . . . You're only detached when it doesn't bother you one way or another."

The secret that Lennier reveals as part of the ceremony is that he loves Delenn. It is a revelation that has been prepared for ever since actor Bill Mumy suggested to Joe Straczynski that Lennier had feelings for Delenn back in Season Two. "If you were to be looking at this from a Lennier perspective, "Quality of Mercy," "Ceremonies of Light and Dark" are probably the two biggest punctuation marks for him," says Bill. "I liked that show a lot. It was flattering to see that something that Joe had allowed me to put in place came to fruition."

The episode also deals with the aftermath of breaking away from Earth. It is not a closed book by any means, and the scene in which the senior officers honor those who died defending the station emphasizes the Human cost of taking that action. There are also housekeeping matters, such as Garibaldi's wiping the computer system of its Earth-controlled command codes. This is a chance to introduce a strong thread of humor as a counterpoint to the drama of "Severed Dreams." When Garibaldi reinstalls the system, he finds he has resurrected the computer's original artificial personality, which turns out to have the voice of *Babylon 5*'s creative consultant, Harlan Ellison. "He came in and did the voice-over stuff when we were all working," remembers Jerry Doyle, who, as Garibaldi, shared all the scenes with the irritable computer. "Somebody could have read it in for him, and he could have looped it in later, but he was down on the set. It was nice for him to do that."

There are also the remnants of Nightwatch on the station to be dealt with. While much of the episode is in a reflective mood, this element provides the action, with the kidnapping of Delenn and her subsequent rescue. "That was a tough one," says John Flinn, who directed the episode. "It was like two o'clock in the afternoon, and I had to get this thing done, and I had a lot of action. Thank God I had two cameras! Everybody listened, everybody knew what we were doing and how much time we'd got to do it, and it just fell together."

It is during this scene that Delenn runs in front of Sheridan and gets stabbed in the back. It is the first time she acts because of her personal feelings for him and not because she believes he has a greater destiny. "It was a huge scene," remembers Mira Furlan, who plays Delenn. "It required many extras and precise movements, and I had to react at a certain point without knowing exactly when the stabbing was going to happen. I had to have this feeling that I was shot from the back—of course, they don't *actually* stab you!"

The trick to convincing the audience she was stabbed was to cut from a shot of the man throwing the knife to one of the knife already in her back. "They glue a little knife on your back in your dress," says Mira. "It's funny, it's all unreal. I was walking around with that knife, and of course, I forgot that the knife was in my back. I'm drinking coffee going, 'Hi, hello,' and people are freaking out!"

Sheridan's response is just as instinctive. He runs after the kidnapper, and as Bruce Boxleitner says, "I get to beat up a guy much smaller than myself."

"The reaction we got from Sheridan was pretty intense," adds John Flinn. "I had so much fun doing that scene, when he catches up to him [the knife thrower]. I had Bruce in there, I said, 'Come on, buddy, let's go,' because he's so good at that stuff. He's so great at these fights; when you let him go, he just has fun and kicks butt."

There is finally a payoff when, at last, Sheridan admits his feelings to Delenn. "I come in there and reveal, more importantly than anything, how much I feel for her," says Bruce. "That's great stuff. You can never miss with that stuff. Shmaltzy, but good."

For Ivanova, her secret is her love for Talia. "That came out of nowhere to me," says actress Claudia Christian. "I thought I was going to tell her that I was a latent telepath or that I was frightened or some Ivanova thing like 'Sometimes I'm scared' or something like that. I was shocked when it was 'I think I loved Talia,' but on the other hand, if that made such an impact on her that she was so confused about it, felt so bad about it, or maybe felt so taken, this was a healing process by admitting that she actually loved this person. It probably made it a little bit easier to swallow, the whole betrayal thing, because she was acting from her heart. Sometimes it's okay to be taken for a ride, if you're acting on your best interests, you were just genuinely loving someone. It's their fault that they screwed you over: it's their fault, it's their incapability of loving, it's their inability to give and to accept your love. So I think by admitting that Ivanova loved Talia, it is a way of healing that whole incident."

The final act is for the command staff to give up their old uniforms, symbolically abandoning their final ties to Earth. When they walk into the Observation Dome in the new uniforms, they are, as Sheridan explains, "reborn." And with a new look, Babylon 5 completes its transition into a new era.

12
"Sic Transit Vir"

Cast

Captain John Sheridan ....Bruce Boxleitner
Commander Susan Ivanova..............Claudia Christian
Security Chief Michael Garibaldi ....Jerry Doyle
Ambassador Delenn ....Mira Furlan
Citizen G'Kar ....Andreas Katsulas
Ambassador Londo Mollari ....Peter Jurasik
Dr. Stephen Franklin ....Richard Biggs
Lennier ....Bill Mumy
Marcus Cole ....Jason Carter
Lyta Alexander ....Patricia Tallman
Vir Cotto ....Stephen Furst

Guest Stars

Centauri Official ....Damian London
Lyndisty ....Carmen Thomas

A pair of bare legs walk into the Observation Dome. "Good morning," says Ivanova cheerfully. All the techs turn and watch her openmouthed as she begins to talk through the business of the day. She stops and looks at them nonplussed. "What?" she asks. Then she looks down at herself—she is totally naked? "Aaarrrgggh!" She wakes up in bed, still screaming. "I hate dreams like that."

Londo shows Vir a surprise that has arrived for him from their homeworld. A beautiful Centauri woman. "Your wife has come all the way here to see you," says Londo with a smile. Vir protests that he is not married. "In a few days, you will be," Londo assures him.

Zack enters C&C carrying a bunch of Narn transit papers that have been approved by someone called "Abrahamo Lincolni." "Since when is that a Centauri name?" exclaims Ivanova. Zack is also suspicious,

*especially because they were issued through Vir's office
on Minbar.*

*Vir sits in the Zen Garden with Lyndisty, his wife-to-
be. She speaks of their life to come as he regards her
with enchanted eyes. She leans over and kisses him
generously on the lips. A wave of unexpected emotion
tingles through his body. "If kisses could kill, that one
would have flattened several small towns," he says,
somewhat breathless. He takes her head in his hands,
pulls her close, and returns the kiss.*

*A Narn pulls a knife from his belt as he sees Vir and
Lyndisty approach. He charges forward, and Vir steps in
to stop him. They wrestle, Vir trying to keep the blade
from his body. The Narn hits him in the stomach, then
across the head, and knocks Vir to the floor. Zack and a
security team approach, PPGs drawn. They order the
Narn to put down his weapon. But he lunges forward,
shouting, "Ragatsa Chon-Kar!" Zack fires, and the
Narn falls down, dead.*

*Chon-Kar is a blood oath. Ivanova believes it has
something to do with the forged Narn transit papers.
The files show that all of the two thousand Narns whose
papers passed through Vir's office are dead. "They're not
dead," Vir protests, explaining that it is a cover story he
fabricated to stop people from looking for them once
they escaped from Narn. "If I hadn't gotten them out,
they would have died."*

*Londo feels slighted by Vir's actions and ensures that
he is removed from his position on Minbar. But Londo
does not know about Abrahamo Lincolni, so travel
papers can still be authorized with that name. Ivanova
decides to keep Vir around for a while and see how
many more Narns he can save. Perhaps doing something
useful will help get rid of her bad dreams.*

*Lyndisty sees that Vir is upset and takes him to her
quarters. She offers him a present to cheer him up—a
Narn, tied up and helpless. She recognized him as an
escapee from her father's extermination program. After
the last war, her father was put in charge of killing*

aggressive Narns to eliminate that part of their character from the gene pool. That is probably why the Narn tried to kill her. Lyndisty takes a knife and hands it to Vir, offering him a chance to take the Narn's life "as a token of my affection for you and a testimony to our marriage."

Lyndisty's parents reconsider the marriage following Vir's demotion, and she has to return home. But before she goes, she kisses Vir softly and promises to wait for him. "I will see you again, Vir," she says. "Soon."

The title of the episode, "Sic Transit Vir," is Latin for "thus passes the man" and indicates that Vir is growing up and taking charge of his own life. After two and a half years of following in Londo's shadow, he makes a decision to help the Narns in his own small way and finds himself in a relationship with a Centauri woman. "It is my favorite episode, of course, because I was the center of both of those," says actor Stephen Furst. "I enjoyed doing it."

Vir was little more than Londo's messenger boy in his early days on Babylon 5. Over time, the two of them became friends, but Londo was still very much in control. Vir gradually gained confidence in speaking out, telling Londo not to order a strike against the Narn in "The Coming of Shadows." He was still under Londo's command, however, and in "A Day in the Strife," Vir goes along with Londo's plans to station him on Minbar even though he does not want to go. By the time we get to "Sic Transit Vir," something has changed. Here is a character who has gained the confidence to act out of his own conscience. "I wasn't surprised that he wanted to help the Narns," says Stephen. "I was surprised that he had enough guts to go out on a limb as far as he did, to disobey Londo and do it behind his back, but 'humanity' was more important to him at that point."

"This is definitely where Vir has evolved a spine," says writer Joe Straczynski. "Vir is a person of good heart, and in a corrupt society like the Centauri society, there isn't much of a venue for that to be expressed. On Minbar, he had the opportunity to do that, and he took it. It was important to take Vir from the very first episode through to the present and show him gradually getting more confident, being able to stand up to Londo and doing what he thinks is right."

Londo, of course, is horrified. Even though he has shown remorse at starting the Narn-Centauri War and has moved to disassociate himself from Morden, he has no sympathy for Vir's actions. "There is nothing that drives him more than his love and his passion for the Centauri," explains Londo actor Peter Jurasik. "For him to see Vir, at least in Londo's mind, turn and make a decision as an individual instead of for his people brings up all the fears within Londo that he hates about himself. He lets Vir know not only is he disapproving of the act itself, but it threatens him—Londo. I believe his outrage is sincere on a lot of levels. He just feels, in a sense, betrayed."

While Vir is at the center of revelations about the Narns he saved, his life is developing on a much more personal level. When he is presented with a woman who is to be his wife, he begins to experience emotions he has not experienced before. These are new feelings for Vir but not a problem for Stephen Furst. "I use something called emotional recall," says the actor. "If I need to be sad or something, I think of something sad in my own life. With that, it was emotional recall again. I would use an instance where I was smitten by someone. It's all make-believe, it's all fake."

There is much that is beautiful about Lyndisty, the woman Vir is due to marry. She is physically attractive and absolutely devoted to Vir, but underneath the veneer of beauty lies something ugly. She talks about Narns being little more than beasts of the field, of mass genocide being "necessary for pacification," and of killing hundreds of them herself. Her attitude is repulsive but sincere. She grew up in a household where her father was in charge of "culling the herds," as she puts it, and that is all she has ever known. She describes killing in poetic terms, remembering Narn villages burning with "flames rising up into the night like brilliant flowers embracing the spring." It expresses the central dichotomy of the character, that inside something so beautiful is something so ugly.

Vir is totally smitten by her and suddenly finds himself in a sexual situation he has no experience of. It is the perfect opportunity for some comedy in distinctive Vir fashion. Unable to turn to Londo for advice, he turns to Ivanova and gets totally flustered trying to explain Centauri sexual anatomy. "I liked that," says actress Claudia Christian. "Working with Stephen is so funny; I think we milked it. At one point, it felt like we were doing Diane Keaton in Woody Allen, this kind of stuttering Woody Allenish kind of acting, which was hysterical. I realized I was beginning to sound like Vir!"

There is a lot of humor in this episode, and it was something director Jesús Treviño particularly wanted to encourage. "I said to Joe and John [Copeland], 'Let's go for some of the inherent humor in this,' and certainly Stephen Furst really came to the party on that one. Both Vir and Londo play so well off each other; they've been doing it for so many years now that there's a great deal of chemistry when you put both of them in a room together. Jurasik himself is so funny as a human being as well; he's always cutting up on the set and kind of informs it with a certain amount of humor. That scene where he was chasing the beetle, he just had the crew in stitches doing different versions of it."

There's more humor with the Sheridan/Delenn relationship. While Vir is trying to deal with the prospect of marriage. Sheridan and Delenn are gently testing the waters regarding their relationship. The scene in which she has dinner at his place is a reversal of the scene in which Sheridan ate a Minbari meal at Delenn's in "Confessions and Lamentations." Both were played for comedy. This scene opens with the camera panning around Sheridan's kitchen, showing it stacked high with dirty kitchenware. Cooking is clearly not Sheridan's forte, something he shares with actor Bruce Boxleitner. "I am at a total loss," says Bruce. "When I was single—oh God, starve to death! I went through all of this stuff to make my own cooking, ate it so fast, and then had an hour's worth of cleaning up afterward. Or I ate half of it while it was in the process, and then I had nothing left. So I was never any good. I have no talent. That's been carried over to Sheridan. He's totally inept."

Then came the scene where Sheridan and Delenn almost kiss but are interrupted by Ivanova. "To Mira and I, being adults, we're looking at this going, 'Oh my God, what is this teasy, childish thing,' and that's where Joe says, 'Remember what I said, Delenn isn't an Earth woman and is not sophisticated in this. For all their sophistication, they're very naive in another way. Also, this is a Minbari woman and an Earth man, no one's ever done this before.' It's like a first, and feeling our way, these almost stolen kisses and all that, still kind of shy about it all."

There was no shyness involved, however, in the scene in which Ivanova walks into C&C naked. Yes, that really is Claudia Christian; she didn't have a stand-in, and, yes, she was wearing virtually nothing. "I had a friend call me one day and say, 'You were just naked on TV,' and I'm like, 'What?' " remembers Claudia. "Joe's very sweet and even in the script it said, 'naked or in a nightgown, whatever I felt comfortable as.' I said, 'It's not funny if it's a nightgown. The whole funny thing about it is that it's naked.' Obviously I'd do it, it wasn't a big deal. So I just taped up my boobs all funny and sloppy, and they shot it from behind. We had fun with it. I'm not particularly shy. I don't have a problem with it; it's not like I showed anything. The crew's seen it all anyway."

Ivanova solves her nightmare problems by doing something positive, helping the fictional Abrahamo Lincolni to rescue Narns. As such, it is the third character thread of the episode. "Sic Transit Vir" is not about furthering the plot; it is about the characters and, as such, forms part of the varied picture that is *Babylon 5*.

13
"A Late Delivery from Avalon"

Cast

Captain John Sheridan	Bruce Boxleitner
Commander Susan Ivanova	Claudia Christian
Security Chief Michael Garibaldi	Jerry Doyle
Ambassador Delenn	Mira Furlan
Citizen G'Kar	Andreas Katsulas
Ambassador Londo Mollari	Peter Jurasik
Dr. Stephen Franklin	Richard Biggs
Lennier	Bill Mumy
Marcus Cole	Jason Carter
Lyta Alexander	Patricia Tallman
Vir Cotto	Stephen Furst

Guest Stars

Emmett Farquaha	Michael Kagan
Arthur	Michael York
Security Guard No. 1	Michael Kelly
Med. Tech.	James Kiriyama-Lem
Old Woman	Dona Hardy
Merchant	Roger Hampton
Lurker	Robert Schuch
Security Guard No. 2	Jerry O'Donnell

A man whips out a sword from under his cloak and points the shining blade at a Babylon 5 security guard. "I am Arthur, son of Uther Pendragon and king of the Britons."

Marcus steps forward and kneels before the man. "Apologies, my lord, we were not notified of your return." He asks Arthur to lower his sword and go with Dr. Franklin. "If you refuse, my friend here will be penalized harshly for failing to obey orders." Arthur smiles and agrees.

Only Marcus believes he could really be King Arthur. If the Vorlons went to Earth and took Arthur out of his time, like they did with Sebastian, he would fit the legend. But Franklin does not believe it. He thinks the man has delusions brought on from trauma or a breakdown. "What terrible thing could have happened to drive him seventeen hundred years into the past to find peace and meaning?" he wonders.

Arthur escapes from Medlab and, wandering around the station, finds an old woman crying in Down Below. Thieves stole the last picture she had of her late husband because the frame was valuable. Arthur takes pity on her and promises to find the men responsible. Before long, he is standing among a gang of lurkers with his sword drawn. "What manner of men prey on the weak and the poor, stealing from old women?" They mock his unlikely threats, and the leader rushes at him with a steel bar. Arthur elbows him in the face and deflects the knife blows of the others. But he is still one man against many, until G'Kar steps into the fray.

Arthur retrieves the picture and returns it to the old woman. Afterward, he celebrates his victory by getting drunk with G'Kar. As they talk, Arthur thinks back to the time when his forces and those of his arch enemy, Mordred, met at Camlann to agree to a truce. "One of Mordred's knights saw an adder about to strike, so he drew his sword," remembers Arthur. "The others saw it, and the killing began."

Using DNA samples, Franklin traces Arthur through EarthForce records and finds that his real name is David McIntyre. He was the gunnery sergeant on the ship that began the Earth-Minbari War. When a Minbari ship approached with its gunports open—a sign of respect— the captain panicked and ordered the crew to open fire. Franklin confronts Arthur with his discovery, and Arthur flashes back to the battle and the moment he pressed the button. "A quarter of a million men and women—dead *on the battlefield at Camlann," Arthur says in pain. But Camlann was not where they died; they died in the Earth-Minbari War.*

Arthur lies in Medlab, clutching the sword that he calls Excalibur, racked by trauma and unable to hide behind the legend of King Arthur any longer. Marcus reflects that the story says Arthur could not be healed until he went full circle, back to where it originally started. Excalibur had to be returned to the Lady of the Lake. That's why he came to Babylon 5.

Ambassador Delenn of the Minbari Federation enters Medlab where Arthur lies. In his mind he sees the outstretched arm of the Lady of the Lake. He gives her Excalibur, and Delenn takes his hand in a symbol of understanding and forgiveness.

G'Kar arranges for Arthur to help in the Narn resistance, convinced of his ability to organize others into something better and nobler. "I am healed, Doctor," Arthur assures Franklin. "Soul and body knitted together. One journey is ended, another beckons."

Many works have had an influence on *Babylon 5*. J. Michael Straczynski admits to being influenced by the myth of the hero, particularly in the writings of Joseph Campbell, and Greek mythology; there are even some subtle references to *The Lord of the Rings*, if you know where to look for them. "A Late Delivery from Avalon" suggests a strong connection with the Arthurian legend, which naturally leads people to wonder how much Arthur has influenced the *Babylon 5* story. "Only tangentially," says the writer. "There're some structural things that you can apply that to. It's more tonality than specifics. The heroic adventure and the transition of someone who doesn't think he may be worthy of the crown being touched by destiny, and then being propelled into a position where he has to achieve that destiny. Sometimes there's a price to pay, such as in the fall of Camelot. So it's a tonality thing and the sense of the heroic tradition, rather than the specifics of Arthur per se."

What marks the episode in the minds of many of the people involved is Michael York, who came in to play folklore legend King Arthur. "Michael York was great, so princely, so kingly," says Jason Carter, who plays Marcus. "It comes from the time when stars crossed over and were perceived as aristocracy, particularly if you've played a lot of aristocracy like he has done, then suddenly you're an ambassador for Britain. I think growing up with him as an image on the screen, it's more powerfully subconsciously effective than you think, and I must admit I was frightened that I wasn't going to be very good after all the films I saw him do when I was growing up."

"It's a constant classroom situation," reflects Richard Biggs. "You bring these people in, and you get to talk to them. You learn more about acting by sitting and talking to people. I remember talking to him and learning even more watching him prepare. The three minutes before the camera starts to roll, watching him going from Michael York to King Arthur. Watching the transformation, watching him prepare, it was quite interesting."

Few of the characters on Babylon 5 actually believe the man could be who he claims, but the slim possibility that he might be King Arthur is kept alive for most of the episode. Franklin relates that the Arthurian legend could have been based on a real person, while Marcus reminds everyone that the Vorlons have been responsible for taking historical figures from Earth, as demonstrated by the arrival of Jack the Ripper in "Comes the Inquisitor."

While such questions about his identity are being asked, he finds an unlikely ally in G'Kar. When Arthur takes up arms against those who prey on the weak, G'Kar steps in, as a further example of his determination following his recent religious experience, to help others. "It wasn't an arc story for Babylon 5, but it's part of G'Kar's arc," says Andreas Katsulas. "Here comes King Arthur, and everybody's going, 'Oh, the guy's loony, thinks he's King Arthur.' G'Kar absolutely accepts him as authentic. It's like a child going to Disneyland and taking Mickey Mouse's hand, and to the child, it *is* Mickey Mouse. He doesn't think there's somebody hiding in a costume. G'Kar's totally open to it. He thinks whatever his problem is, it doesn't matter, he's got a good heart. G'Kar jumps right off the balcony and starts slaying dragons with him."

Afterward, they get drunk together, allowing Arthur to reveal more of his legendary story to someone who accepts it at face value. It is also a chance for the audience to see G'Kar, the noble Narn, totally inebriated. Drunken deeds are often used to add humor to a story but tend to work only if the actor can carry it off convincingly. Andreas Katsulas, of course, did so admirably. "I'm not a drinker," he says. "I think, back in my twenties in college, I got drunk once and saw that it was not for me. Does the guy playing Othello need to have killed someone to know how to play the part? No. I faked it! I kind of slurred and just acted drunk; it was like a kid would do it."

"Arthur" turns out not to be the legendary king of the Britons but a wounded soldier who seeks refuge in the legend to escape his pain. That inner turmoil is not implied or talked about but shown visually through the use of black-and-white sequences that juxtapose images from Arthurian legend, the Earth-Minbari War, and an unending corridor. "We wanted to get the feeling, as was written, that it was a very long corridor, limbolike, that had doorways to this other dimension," explains director Mike Vejar. "This character was forced to run up and down forever and open doors to the things that frightened him most. It was really fun to shoot. As far as the practical shooting of it, they took the Central Corridor and built a diminishing-scale set. The size of the doors diminished toward the background, and we cloaked the whole thing in black to create the image of limbo and shot it at different frame rates than the normal twenty-four frames. We shot it six frames a second, and then printed every frame four times, so that gave it a normal-speed feel but very jerky. The camera we used is called a ramp camera. We ramped from six frames a second to, I think, one hundred and twenty frames a second, so it got that real jerky thing, and then it started to float into a very slow-motion thing. I thought it was quite effective in getting the nightmare flavor of running forever and not being able to get where you think you want to go."

Once again, an episode brings the Earth-Minbari War into focus, a part of the *Babylon 5* back story that continues to influence current events, even though it ended twelve years ago. "It was a pivotal event," says Joe Straczynski. "It's like people ten years after World War II talking about it. It was the seminal event in the lives of most Humans in the time of the story, and things aren't just forgotten. There's a line in a much later episode which says, 'The duration is going to last a lot longer than the war,' and the implication that I'm trying to go after here and elsewhere is, in television, once the war's over we never think about it again, but in real life, things have ways of hanging about and there are long-term emotional and personal consequences that have to be dealt with. That's why, even after the Shadow War is eventually over, that isn't the end of the series. The series will go on for a certain period beyond that to show the consequences. Again, choices, responsibilities, and consequences. That to me is the more interesting stuff—the process and the results. To show that pain does not end when the treaty is signed."

The episode ends with Marcus talking to Franklin, trying to make a correlation between the people on the station and the figures from the Arthurian myth. As he matches up Kosh to Merlin, Franklin to Perceval, and himself to Galahad, it is almost like eavesdropping on a fan's conversation. "By this point, I had heard enough on the Net and seen the fan reaction to know that they were trying to find some template that they could stick *Babylon 5* into," says Joe. "They don't do it with print fiction, but they tend to do it with television fiction, thinking 'What is it like?' SF fans often say, 'We want something different,' and then you give them something different and they want to make it like what they had before. They want a paradigm they can relate to. Having seen this enough times and having seen none of them go after Arthur,

I thought I'd lob a grenade in this, 'Here Arthur, go ahead, go nuts with this one!' When it came out, people said, 'Well, maybe he is doing Arthur,' and started looking for all those correlations, which really aren't there. I figured, 'If you're going to have fun with me, I'm going to have some fun with you.' "

14
"Ship of Tears"

Cast

Captain John Sheridan ....Bruce Boxleitner
Commander Susan Ivanova ....Claudia Christian
Security Chief Michael Garibaldi ....Jerry Doyle
Ambassador Delenn ....Mira Furlan
Citizen G'Kar ....Andreas Katsulas
Ambassador Londo Mollari ....Peter Jurasik
Dr. Stephen Franklin ....Richard Biggs
Lennier ....Bill Mumy
Marcus Cole ....Jason Carter
Lyta Alexander ....Patricia Tallman
Vir Cotto ....Stephen Furst

Guest Stars

Bester ....Walter Koenig
Carolyn ....Joan McMurtrey

While Sheridan is out testing the station's new range of Starfuries, ships able to operate inside a planet's atmosphere, he detects another vessel. It is Bester, the Psi Cop. "I have something for you, Captain," he says. "Something very important."

It is time to tell G'Kar the truth. He helped the station when it broke away from Earth, and now, as agreed, he is to join the War Council. But first Delenn has to tell him that she knew about the Shadows before they attacked Narn and said nothing. Tears form in Delenn's eyes as she explains that it was necessary to sacrifice millions of his people to save billions. "You have come a long way, G'Kar. Someday, when all this is over, perhaps you will find it in your heart to forgive me."

He looks back at her, almost overcome with emotion. "Perhaps," he says, "but not today."

Bester says he knows the Shadows are influencing

President Clark back on Earth. They have infiltrated the Psi Corps and have plans for his telepaths. He has heard that a vessel is delivering weapon components to the Shadows through hyperspace and wants Sheridan's help to intercept it. Sheridan, although still distrustful of Bester, allows him to board the White Star and use his telepathic skills to lead them to the vessel. The White Star grabs it with a magnetic field, but sensors detect an approaching Shadow ship. They prepare to fight, but inexplicably, the ship breaks off and lets them return to Babylon 5.

The Earth vessel is full of cryonic sleeper tubes containing telepaths with cyberweb implants protruding from their brains and a look of terror frozen on their faces. Franklin brings one of them—a woman named Carolyn—out of suspended animation.

Carolyn takes over Medlab, wrapping energy and information cables around her as she plugs herself into the space station control systems. Franklin enters with Garibaldi and Bester. On seeing Bester, she calls to him, "Alfred . . . help me." He steps into the light, and it illuminates his Psi Corps badge. She panics, blasting a bolt of energy across the room. "The sign hurts us," she says, "we cannot hear the machine . . ." Franklin approaches her and injects her with a sedative.

Carolyn is one of the "weapon components" Bester told them about, telepaths who were to form the central operating cores of Shadow vessels. She is also Bester's lover. He helped her when she refused to take sleepers or join the Corps, and then she became pregnant with his child. "She's the only thing I have left," Bester tells Sheridan. "If it means you can save her, I'll do anything you want to help."

G'Kar enters the war room as a full member of the War Council, with Sheridan, Delenn, and Ivanova. Sitting at the table is Garibaldi, gleefully tapping his fingers on the Book of G'Quan. He opens the Narn holy book and asks G'Kar to read. "And the spirit of darkness moved upon the land. It screamed in the *dreams of the mindwalkers, and they fell, destroyed by it. Until it was driven out by G'Quan and the last surviving mindwalkers." It explains why the Shadows did not attack the White Star when Bester was onboard and why Carolyn lashed out at the Psi Corps symbol. The Shadows are afraid of telepaths, or "mindwalkers." The telepaths must be able to break the mental connection between a Shadow vessel and its living central core. Sheridan senses a hope that he has not felt in a long time.*

"We've got a weapon," he says. "My God, people, we've got a weapon!"

"My favorite episode by far," says Walter Koenig enthusiastically. "It really was multidimensional."

Walter Koenig's character, Bester, had been introduced in the first season as a representative of the dark side of the Psi Corps. He began very much as the villain, but in the third season, Bester is revealed to be far more complex. Here we learn that he is in love with a woman who is expecting his child and whom he helps even though she is a blip, a telepath who refuses to join the Psi Corps or take sleeper drugs. "The problem was reconciling this other side of him with what had gone before," says Walter. "I had to reevaluate who the character was. What made it possible for me to play—with what I hope was honesty—was that I concluded that there isn't anybody who hasn't some compassion or sensitivity in them, even if it has been repressed or destroyed or blunted or very controlled. You don't show that face, but it's there. I don't want to start naming notorious people in history because it's so offensive to name them and say that they probably had a touching side, but the fact of the matter is—and here, I'm going to do it—the Jeffrey Dahmers and the Adolf Hitlers had their moments. I decided Bester was not just a bad guy. We got an opportunity to see that he could be very destructive and very malevolent, and at the same time, he could have a great love and could have a great sense of tenderness for somebody."

It is not a reversal but a broadening of the character. His

malevolent side never disappears, and the audience is reminded of that in the first scene he has with Ivanova. In what is a wonderful excuse to shut two characters who hate each other into a room together, Ivanova meets Bester alone to assess if he will keep his promise not to scan them. In this scene, Bester tells Ivanova that she has her mother's eyes, suggesting he was involved in the treatment that led her to commit suicide. "That was a fun scene," says Walter. "It was a fun scene because some of it doesn't really have to do with plot. I started quoting from "The Cask of Amontillado." What the hell did that have to do with the plot? It didn't, but it had to do with character, and that's a luxury. For example, when I was on *Star Trek*, my role on the show was expository, to give information about the plot, and in that regard, there's very little opportunity for character; it's simply you are a device, you are a tool. But Joe writes for the character so you get to be a human being."

The title "Ship of Tears" relates to the horror of the Human telepaths being transported to the Shadows, but it can also relate, metaphorically, to Babylon 5 itself. For Bester, it is the emotion of knowing what has happened to his beloved Carolyn. For G'Kar, it is discovering that the Minbari knew of the Shadows' plans before they attacked Narn, and for Delenn, it is the pain involved in telling him. That scene was so powerful that the actors did more than portray the emotions of their characters, they experienced them.

"I'll tell you the truth," says Andreas Katsulas, who plays G'Kar. "I felt so strongly about that scene I was in tears from the beginning of that day, every single time we did it, and the tears weren't reserved for the end of the scene. I don't think she [Mira Furlan, Delenn] was expecting that level of emotion from me because we didn't work on it. That's the thing you can't determine, you can't say, "I will be overwhelmed by emotion," because it may not happen. So I don't think she was prepared to feel this, but it overcame her, and I got her going with me in this emotional direction, and those tears at the end from her [were real]. Finally, after four hours of gut-wrenching feeling from me, the director said, "Well, we should have one where you're not all that [emotional]," and that's the one they kept, where they just allowed a little emotion at the end. They had take after take of raw feeling, but they wanted the tear from her; they didn't want it from G'Kar."

"I just admire Andreas so much," adds Mira. "He inspires me; he also intimidates me by the quality of his work. But here we really clicked, I think. There was something going on which was completely different to what we were planning. There is the dialogue and you play the content of the scene, but there is this whole layer underneath with all these feelings—incredible pain. Somehow he provoked an incredible pain within himself and within me, and it was just happening. He just opened something within both of us, which I think was one of the best moments for me in terms of working with the other actor. It was so easy, because once it happens, you just let it go, and you follow that track and you surrender yourself to that feeling. It's like an emotional ball that you keep throwing and catching. It's a wonderful thing. It rarely happens, though. When I think about my whole career and all the movies that I did and all the plays, I had a couple of moments like that with other actors, and for me, this is what I enjoy, this is when it really pays off."

Once G'Kar has been told what Delenn and the others have been hiding from him, he takes the final step and joins them in the war room. This is the first time we see the set, marking a change not only in G'Kar's role but also in the direction of Babylon 5, as it prepares to make a stand against the Shadows. It is a key moment, and director Mike Vejar had a definite idea of how he wanted to shoot it. "I wanted the audience to feel everything G'Kar was feeling when he was taken into this room for the first time," he says. "As I recall, we shot it with a steadicam and followed G'Kar, taking in the room as G'Kar would. The camera was playing the same emotion of revealing the wonder of seeing that room for the first time."

Throughout the first three-quarters of the season, there is a growing sense that G'Kar is underestimated by the others. As Sheridan points out early in this episode, G'Kar was the first one to warn him about the Shadows, long before Delenn said anything. And it is G'Kar—through the Book of G'Quan that he gave to Garibaldi—who finally gives them something to use as a weapon against the enemy. Telepaths, the book reveals, helped drive the Shadows from Narn in the previous war. It explains Carolyn's instinctive fear of the Psi Corps symbol, but moreover, it brings together many of the disparate story threads that have been building in *Babylon 5* right from the beginning. It explains that Narn telepaths disappeared a thousand years ago because they were destroyed by the Shadows in the last war, and it explains why the Vorlons engineered the emergence of Human telepaths, which were first detected at the beginning of the twenty-second century. This fact touches many aspects of the plot, from the foundation of the Psi Corps to the Narns' quest for telepathic genetic material, and reveals the activities of the Vorlons and the Shadows. It demonstrates the complexity of J. Michael Straczynski's story arc, in that all these diverse elements were derived from one single plot point. "That's why I had telepaths there in the first place," he confirms. "The whole theory is that telepaths, as somebody even points out, came out a hundred years before—give or take—and that was due to the Vorlon interference. So the logical question is why were they created and why were they corrupted? That premise goes back to the pilot; that's why I had them there. If they weren't going to be used in the Shadow War, they wouldn't be in the story at all."

15
"Interludes and Examinations"

Cast

Captain John Sheridan	Bruce Boxleitner
Commander Susan Ivanova	Claudia Christian
Security Chief Michael Garibaldi	Jerry Doyle
Ambassador Delenn	Mira Furlan
Citizen G'Kar	Andreas Katsulas
Ambassador Londo Mollari	Peter Jurasik
Dr. Stephen Franklin	Richard Biggs
Lennier	Bill Mumy
Marcus Cole	Jason Carter
Lyta Alexander	Patricia Tallman
Vir Cotto	Stephen Furst

Guest Stars

Dr. Hobbs	Jennifer Balgobin
Morden	Ed Wasser
Brakiri	Jonathan Chapman
Adira (in flashback)	Fabiana Udenio
Refa (in flashback)	William Forward
David Sheridan	Rance Howard

The Shadows are attacking openly for the first time. The Brakiri is one of the races being threatened, but their closest potential ally, the Gaim, is refusing to get involved. "The enemy is powerful," the Gaim ambassador tells Sheridan. "Show us you have equal power, then we will consider."

Dr. Franklin orders an alien patient's lung to be ventilated, telling the medtechs to stop at nine psi. Dr. Hobbs protests, but Franklin will have none of it. "What the hell is it with everybody in this room?" he yells, enraged. "I said thirteen psi. Thirteen! Thirteen! Thirteen!"

Garibaldi, having witnessed Franklin's outburst, considers checking blood samples stored in the Medlab computer for stim levels. But Franklin reveals he has already run the tests. "Figured I'd show you," he says. "Prove that you were wrong." But Garibaldi is not wrong. Franklin is addicted to stims.

Morden faces Londo in the corridor. "Somehow you've convinced your government to pull back their campaign against several other worlds," says Morden. "We need your government to continue its campaign." But Londo has no desire to help him. He has other things on his mind—Lady Adira is returning.

Londo stands in the customs area, clutching a bunch of starlace flowers. "I feel happy," he says, barely able to catch his breath. "I had almost forgotten what it was like." Londo looks for Adira in the crowd of people stepping off the newly arrived transport, but she does not appear. His excitement falls away as he sees the medtechs bring out a stretcher. Londo realizes the dead woman is Adira, and the starlaces slip from his fingers.

Londo does not see Morden pay off a man who was on the same transport as Adira. He believes it was Refa who had her killed and decides to reestablish his links with Morden: "You said you would go away for as long as I wanted. I no longer want that," says Londo. "The only thing I want now is revenge."

Sheridan tells Kosh that many of the other races are refusing to join the war because they can see no chance of winning. If the Vorlons enter just one fight against the Shadows, it would give the others hope. Kosh refuses and walks away. "Don't turn your back on me!" says Sheridan, and he stands in Kosh's way. "You wanted to teach me to fight legends; well you're a legend, too, and I'm not going away until you agree." Kosh's eye lens widens, and a burst of unseen energy slams Sheridan up against the wall. Sheridan comes back at him relentlessly. "Ships, colonies, whole worlds are being destroyed out

*there, while you do nothing. How many more have to
die before you're satisfied?" Sheridan is whipped
backward by Kosh's power and held there by the throat.
"Go ahead," Sheridan says, struggling for breath.
"Maybe one more death will balance out the books."*

*Kosh releases him, and Sheridan clutches his neck. "I
will do as you ask," says Kosh. "But there is a price to
pay. I will not be there to help you when you go to
Z'ha'dum."*

*The Vorlons engage the Shadows, and their victory is
decisive enough to persuade the Gaim and others to join
the fight. That night Sheridan dreams of his father, who
tells him he was right. "Don't blame yourself for what
happened later," says the old man. He weakens, and
Sheridan reaches out to catch him. "As long as you're
here, I will always be here."*

*"Kosh!" cries Sheridan, sitting bolt upright in bed. He
knows the Vorlon is dead.*

"Interludes and Examinations" begins with a segment
from Ivanova's personal diary overlaid across a series of
images of everyday events on the station. It was a method
of storytelling that became more common toward the end of
the third season and into the fourth, as the audience needed
to be kept abreast of the increasingly complex storyline.
"One of the things I really enjoyed with that episode was the
opening teaser," says director Jesús Treviño. "It allowed me
to try out something that I'd wanted to do for a long time,
which was do a series of wipes that gets us from one scene
to the other. I storyboarded the thing, so we really had a
sense of how one scene led into another. I thought that was
somewhat metaphorical. It's not often that you get the
chance to have the *form* of what you're doing resonate with
the *content* of what you're doing. But in that particular case,
it really called for a series of seamless transitions that
echoes the fact that we're going somewhere. There's all
these different things in concert, and somehow they're all
kind of taking us there."

The title "Interludes and Examinations" suggests a respite

from the escalating war, the telling of several individual stories that take a closer look at the situation on Babylon 5. In
that sense it is deceptive, because the individual stories
have a significant effect on the direction of the show.

Such is the case with Franklin's story. It is clear to the
audience by this point that he is addicted to stims. He virtually admitted as much to Delenn in "Ceremonies of Light and
Dark." But he is still in denial, and the effects of trying to
deny his addiction begin to show here. He makes a mistake
that nearly kills a patient and takes it out on his staff. It is
only when he is faced with indisputable medical facts, however, that he realizes he must face up to his problem. "I think
if you have an addiction, it usually takes more than people
saying, 'You have an addition,' for you to say, 'Ah, you're
right,' " explains Franklin actor Richard Biggs. "It usually
takes some kind of fall; you fall down some way, you hit rock
bottom, something happens, or almost happens, that either
slaps you in the face or wakes you up. There was an actor,
Kelsey Grammer, who was in a car accident, and he was
drunk, which made him go into some kind of [alcoholic reha-
bilitation] program. That accident, that near-death kind of a
thing, where you go, 'I almost died, maybe I do have a
problem,' was like what happened to Dr. Franklin when he
almost lost that patient. That's the moment when the Doc
goes, 'Oh, my gosh, what would have happened if . . . ?' "

By the end of that little interlude and the examination of
Franklin, he has resigned from his position in preparation for
the "walkabout" thread, which plays out toward the end of
the season. Similarly, Londo's story seems, at first, to be a
vignette. The pressures and the guilt of starting the war are
brushed aside as he anticipates the arrival of Adira Tyree,
the woman he fell in love with in Season One's "Born to the
Purple." Then tragedy strikes. She is killed, and Londo takes
a step backward by turning back to Morden. "It's an interesting place where it drives him because Morden becomes
his source of power," says actor Peter Jurasik. "It harkens
back to the fact that Londo is drawn to power and evil. There
are a lot of places he could pull out, but the card he does
play is revenge, payback, really throwing in fully with the

Shadows and Morden. It's very revealing for who Londo really is. Power versus people is what it's really about, and he will not be outflanked."

The most significant interlude of the episode, however, is Sheridan's attempt to get some of the minor races to join in the fight against the Shadows. He gets what he wants but at a price: the death of Kosh.

Sheridan's confrontation with Kosh in the hallway is an explosive tussle of wills. For Bruce Boxleitner it meant acting with what is, in effect, a walking costume, and he is full of praise for Jeffery Willerth, the man inside. "In every scene I do with Kosh, Jeffrey gets in there and learns it and rehearses, so I actually had somebody there. Ardwight Chamberlain does the voice, but I sometimes feel a little slighted for Jeffrey because he's really acting, and he really gives something back for me to work with. It was quite challenging, and I was very exhausted by the end of that because I had to slam myself around."

The scene is quite long in television terms and steadily builds from normal conversation to anger, until it seems that Kosh is almost ready to kill Sheridan. Hitting the right level of intensity at the right time is the key to getting the maximum impact from a scene. "In first rehearsals, I like taking it as far as it can go," says Bruce. "Where I know how far I can go, where it's too much, and then back off from it. I always find it harder to work up to. I was almost hoarse by the end of it because I was shouting at the top of my lungs. Then we go, 'Okay, let's bring it back and let it build again.' I had to get to a certain point; you had to start at A to get to Z. So it takes a bit of fine-tuning and a number of takes. There were a lot of takes. I was pretty happy with that, and I know Joe was very happy with that. He's not one to compliment anybody, there are very few times, but he just happened to say in passing, 'Good scene with Kosh.' That's his way. Silence would have not been good."

This encounter shows Kosh and the Vorlons in a very different light, capable of anger and of violence. Moments later, that is juxtaposed with Sheridan's dream, where Kosh appears as his father, apologizing to Sheridan and admitting that he was afraid. It is a very touching scene that makes his death all the more shocking because it makes Kosh almost Human. We had already seen Sheridan's feelings for his father in "Severed Dreams," and Kosh takes advantage of that. Even at the last, he does not appear as himself but as an image to manipulate Sheridan's emotions.

Joe Straczynski had not originally planned to kill off Kosh in "Interludes and Examinations." The Vorlon's death was scheduled for later on in the season, as part of a different story thread that led to his assassination. But when Joe set to work on the episode, something was nagging at the back of his mind. It was as if the character were saying to him that he should be killed off now. Following the *Babylon 5* philosophy of choices, consequences, and responsibilities, Kosh was in line to pay for not getting involved in the war at an earlier stage. The argument was that this was the right time to kill off Kosh because it would be more interesting dramatically. It was an argument that Joe, at first, resisted. "I had really not been looking forward to offing Kosh," he says. "I had grown quite fond of him, and when I began writing that episode, the character began poking the back of my head, saying, 'No, do it now for the reason I just expressed,' and I said, 'I don't know—later, later is better. I don't want to do this now.' He said, 'No, you've got to do this now because this is the right time—you know this is the right time, and I know it's the right time.' Writers are schizoids, you've got to understand that. When you have more than one person living in your own head, something is fundamentally wrong. Finally, I said, 'Okay, I'll go with you for now, and we'll see where this goes.' I began taking that direction, and it was, indeed, the right thing to do. The character was right, or that part of my brain that pretended to be the character for the purposes of that conversation was correct."

16
"War Without End," Part 1

Cast

Captain John Sheridan ....Bruce Boxleitner
Commander Susan Ivanova ....Claudia Christian
Security Chief Michael Garibaldi ....Jerry Doyle
Ambassador Delenn ....Mira Furlan
Citizen G'Kar ....Andreas Katsulas
Ambassador Londo Mollari ....Peter Jurasik
Dr. Stephen Franklin ....Richard Biggs
Lennier ....Bill Mumy
Marcus Cole ....Jason Carter
Lyta Alexander ....Patricia Tallman
Vir Cotto ....Stephen Furst

Guest Stars

Rathenn ....Time Winters
Ambassador Jeffrey Sinclair ....Michael O'Hare
Tech ....Joshua Cox
Zathras...Tim Choate
Spragg...Eric Zivot
Major Krantz (in flashback)...............Kent Broadhurst
Centauri Guard ....Kevin Fry

A Minbari runs through the temple, calling after the hooded figure ahead of him. He is holding a casket that had been locked away for nine hundred years, until today, when the ancient books said it should be opened. The hooded figure lifts the lid. Inside is a letter with his name on it: Jeffrey David Sinclair.

Babylon 5 is picking up a distress signal from Sector 14 where Babylon 4 disappeared through time. "They're killing us," cries a voice. "Can you hear me?

They're killing us." It is Ivanova's voice, and Garibaldi believes it comes from the future—Babylon 5's future.

Sheridan looks up as the doors to the war room open, and Ambassador Sinclair—once Commander Sinclair— walks down the steps. "You've done a good job looking after the place," the ambassador tells his successor.

Delenn urges them all to go to the White Star, where she shows them a visual record of the last great war with the Shadows. The wall behind her shimmers and shows the image of a faltering Minbari fleet. Into that chaos of a thousand years ago, a new base of operations appears. Sheridan stares at it in astonishment. It is Babylon 4. The Shadows recognize Babylon 4's importance and attempt to destroy it, but they are stopped by another ship—the White Star. Sheridan cannot believe it. "Delenn, the question of who stole Babylon 4 is the biggest mystery of the last decade. And now you're telling me that it was me? Is me? Is going to be me?"

"She's telling the truth, Captain," says Sinclair. "If we don't go along with this, we'll change history, and the Shadows will come out of the last war stronger than they should be." And, in their next attack, they will destroy Babylon 5.

Zathras joins the White Star from Epsilon 3, and Sinclair instantly recognizes him as the same alien he saw on Babylon 4 over two years ago. As they prepare to enter the time rift in Sector 14, Zathras hands out time stabilizers to all of them.

A white glow of energy ripples over the White Star as it enters the time rift, where Shadow fighters are escorting a fusion bomb toward Babylon 4. The White Star fires, splitting a fighter into tiny pieces. It deflects and avoids return fire, and closes in. The White Star fires a battery of pulses, until, at last, one of them hits home. The bomb ruptures with a blast of energy, flooding the bridge with the devastating brightness of a thermonuclear explosion. The White Star tries to pull away, but it is caught in the shock wave, which strikes Sheridan's time stabilizer. Delenn cries out, but Marcus *holds her back, as energy writhes through Sheridan's body and he disappears. "He is unstuck in time," says Zathras.*

Sheridan slumps to the floor, his hands tied behind his back. Someone's foot kicks him hard in the stomach, and he is dragged to his feet. He is in the Centauri palace, facing an old Emperor Londo. Sheridan, also older, beaten and confused, stares uncomprehendingly at him. "During your little war, you drove away the Shadows, oh yes," says Londo with disdain. "But you did not think to clean up your mess." Centauri guards drag him across the room and shove him up against the window. Sheridan looks out onto a blackened landscape of burning buildings and heaps of rubble. "There's the legacy of your war," says Londo—a devastated Centauri Prime.

When Commander Sinclair left Babylon 5 to train the Rangers on Minbar, he left behind some loose ends in the storyline. Actor Michael O'Hare had left the series on good terms and always said he would return to conclude that story. More than a year and a half later, that is exactly what he did.

The meeting of the two commanders finally brings together the two phases of the show: the first phase led by Michael O'Hare's Sinclair and the second led by Bruce Boxleitner's Sheridan. In one sense, it is the formal handover from one to the other that we did not get to see when the actors swapped places at the beginning of the second season. Sinclair's line, "You've done a good job looking after the place," is clearly an acknowledgement of that. It was an auspicious moment for the show and was so anticipated that Bruce Boxleitner was aware of a false impression building up in his mind. "I had to face this ghost or this demon, whatever you want to call it, who was there since day one when I walked in," he says. "Michael O'Hare, when I first came aboard, was eight feet tall!"

But any anxiety evaporated when the two lead actors finally got to work together. "We got on famously, we really did. There was no problem whatsoever, and I think people were looking for one—"Is there going to be conflict?" No. No, no, no, no no. We went about the job at hand."

Their first meeting was low-key, almost by accident, and helped set the easy tone with which they worked together. "I had wrapped a scene, and he was just coming in," remembers Bruce. "There was no one else around. I was coming out the door, and as I was heading out, I was undoing my collar, trying to get out of wardrobe and get home, and he walked in and said, 'Bruce—Michael O'Hare.' I said, 'Michael, how are you? Hi.' And we stood there and talked for a few minutes and talked about the upcoming episode. He was there to do some fittings and stuff like that, and it was just like two actors, two friendly guys. We talked and talked and talked. Maybe, for a little bit, it was a little strange, because I felt for him in a way. It had to be a hard thing to do because of all the speculation, the whys and the wherefores. But you know what? It came down to it and we got on with the job and we sat and did it, and I think he enjoyed himself a great deal. I certainly enjoyed it."

"It was fine," says Michael O'Hare. "It was particularly good to see John Flinn, whom I'm particularly fond of, who's director of photography. I like him very much and admire him, so it was good to see him and work with him. I like Bruce very much, a good fellow. I had a lot of other things on my mind, so I just came and did the job and left. It was a little eerie, a little unusual, but it was okay. People were very friendly. It went without a hitch."

"War Without End" is a follow-up to Season One's "Babylon Squared." That first episode elaborated on the mystery of what happened to Babylon 4, introduced the question of The One that Zathras pointed to in the blue spacesuit, and showed the face of an older Sinclair, apparently inside that same blue suit. In writing the first episode, J. Michael Straczynski worked out exactly how the second half of the story would be told. But that was back in the days before Sheridan. When he came to write "War Without End," there was a new captain at the helm. He refuses to say, however, how he would have told the story without

Sheridan. "I'm fundamentally busy enough telling the story that is, without telling the story that isn't or might have been. All I can say is that had Sinclair stayed, a character like Sheridan, or Sheridan himself in a different venue, would have had to come into the story at this point. That is one of the reasons why the change was done when it was done, because the more you sit and think about it, the more you begin to realize that if you develop a character as your lead for three years and then you yank him out, you've got a serious problem on your hands. People may not react well to that. It's better to make that change earlier on than pull the final trigger on it later. The plan was that Sinclair was going to become Valen, that was set up as far away as the first season, so someone like Sheridan would always had to have been there, maybe in a slightly different guise."

Much of the first installment of this two-parter is concerned with setting the scene for the momentous events that happen in the second part. Joe Straczynski felt it was necessary to build a lot of exposition into the plot because so much that happened in "Babylon Squared" was vital to understanding "War Without End." "A lot of folks came to the show in the second season, and they [television stations] weren't running the first season, so a large portion of our audience had never seen the first episode," he says. "You really had to take extraordinary steps to bring people up to speed. It wasn't difficult for me, because I knew the characters and the story pretty well, but I did feel you needed to have a fair amount of exposition there for the viewers who hadn't seen the first season."

Mira Furlan, as Delenn, had the job of explaining much of what had gone before. It was a lot of complex information that was compressed into a small space, and it took her a while to make sense of it all. "I had to go back into old scripts and read it and figure it all out," she says. "That was really, really complicated. You have to be aware of many elements, you have to know the story, you have to be able to connect all the parts and to think in advance and remember what happened. So it was tough, a lot of explaining. I prefer episodes where things are happening, where things are not being explained. For me, as an actor explaining, there's not much you can do. It's the function that has to be done. You have to explain some things, so you do it, but there is no particular depth or drama in it, nothing you can do to contribute somehow."

The secondary effect of putting across all this information is to increase the tension. In fact, most of the first episode is about building expectations for the second part. The message from the future, which says that Babylon 5 is on the brink of destruction, is part of that. It had been heavily foreshadowed by the Centauri seer in "Signs and Portents" and Garibaldi's flashforward in "Babylon Squared," but now the possibility is much closer. Ivanova's desperate call for help from C&C, with the station falling apart all around her, is dated only eight days into the future. "That was interesting to do," says Claudia Christian. "I felt like it was like one of those *Die Hard* movies. I was actually standing on my knees, so that was kind of funny."

But "War Without End" is not just about tying up plot lines from the past: it takes advantage of the instability of time around Babylon 4 to tease the audience with what might happen in the future. Just as the crew of the *White Star* heads to Babylon 4 to resolve the mysteries of "Babylon Squared," another mystery is thrown into the ring. Sheridan is pulled into a future where he is Londo's prisoner and Centauri Prime lies in ruins. The episode was originally going to end there, with Emperor Londo welcoming Sheridan back from the abyss with the words, ". . . just in time to die." But there was so much material in the second episode that some scenes were moved forward, and the audience got to see a couple of extra sequences before the picture froze and revealed that the story was "to be continued . . ."

17
"War Without End,"
Part 2"

Cast

Captain John Sheridan ....Bruce Boxleitner
Commander Susan Ivanova ....Claudia Christian
Security Chief Michael Garibaldi ....Jerry Doyle
Ambassador Delenn ....Mira Furlan
Citizen G'Kar ....Andreas Katsulas
Ambassador Londo Mollari ....Peter Jurasik
Dr. Stephen Franklin ....Richard Biggs
Lennier ....Bill Mumy
Marcus Cole ....Jason Carter
Lyta Alexander ....Patricia Tallman
Vir Cotto ....Stephen Furst

Guest Stars

Rathenn (in flashback) ....Time Winters
Ambassador Jeffrey Sinclair ....Michael O'Hare
Zathras..Tim Choate
Major Krantz ....Kent Broadhurst
Centauri Guard ....Kevin Fry
B4 First Officer ....Bruce Morrow
B4 Security Guard (in flashback).............Frank Costa
The Soul Hunter (in flashback) ..W. Morgan Sheppard
Neroon (in flashback) ....John Vickery

Delenn enters Sheridan's cell on Centauri Prime and reaches out to him. "Our son is safe, John," she says, looking into his confused eyes. "I love you." She pulls him close and kisses him. Passionately. Desperately.

Sheridan gently pulls her away, telling her he has come from the past. Delenn searches his face and sees that it is true. He does not know what happened during

the war. He still has much pain and grief to live through.
"We created something that will endure for a thousand
years," she tells him. "But the price, John, the terrible,
terrible price . . ."

Sheridan and Delenn are brought into the Centauri
palace, where they find Emperor Londo, drunk. It is the
only way to put his "keeper" to sleep for a few minutes,
he tells them. He leans forward to show them the small
dormant creature attached to his neck. He offers them a
chance to escape if they agree to help free his people.

As Sheridan and Delenn rush out, G'Kar enters from
behind. "We have unfinished business between us,
G'Kar," says Londo. "Let us make an end to it . . ."
G'Kar puts his hands around Londo's neck and starts to
strangle the life out of him. Suddenly, Londo's keeper
awakes, and despite himself, Londo lifts his hands to
G'Kar's neck. Moments later, when Vir walks in, both of
them are dead. Vir sadly picks up the fallen seal of the
emperor.

Pain shoots through Sheridan as he feels himself being
pulled back through time. "Take these words back with
you to the past," Delenn says urgently. "Do not go to
Z'ha'dum."

Sheridan materializes into a blue spacesuit, on which
Zathras has attached the damaged time stabilizer. But
when the suit's powerpack fades, Sheridan becomes
unstuck in time again and appears in Babylon 4's
Central Corridor. His shimmering image is what the
younger Sinclair and Garibaldi saw when they visited
the station two years ago. Zathras tells them, "It is The
One." Zathras drops a mended time stabilizer into his
hands and the blue-suited figure disappears.

Babylon 4 has become unstable because of the time-
travel equipment fitted to it. The younger Sinclair and
Garibaldi race to leave the station with the Babylon 4
command staff and Zathras. The whole place shakes. A
structural beam is dislodged and knocks Zathras to the
ground. As he lies trapped, a blue-suited figure
approaches. "Zathras knew you would not leave him,"

he says. "Zathras trusts The One." The figure removes
its helmet and looks down at Zathras. It is Delenn.

Zathras, Delenn, Sheridan, and Ambassador Sinclair
meet up at C&C on Babylon 4. Sinclair does not
understand why "The One" Zathras pointed to was
Delenn. Zathras tells Sinclair: "You are The One who
was." Then turns to Delenn: "You are The One
who is." And finally, to Sheridan: "You are The One
who will be."

Sinclair knows he must be the one to stay behind on
Babylon 4 and take it back into the past. That is what he
was told by the letter he received on Minbar, a letter he
wrote to himself—or will write—nine hundred years
ago. The Minbari will not accept the station with a
Human on board, so he uses a triluminary to spin a
chrysalis, like the one Delenn used to become half
Human. When he arrives in the past, his appearance is
that of a Minbari. "I am called Valen," he tells those
who come to meet him, "and we have much work ahead
of us."

Sheridan is thrust into a nightmare when time pulls him
forward into the future. But in the middle of all this
horror, he has a moment of tenderness with Delenn. At last,
after more than a year of building the relationship between
these two people, they kiss. "It's a desperate one if you'll
notice, because we're about to be taken out and may be
executed," says Bruce Boxleitner. "It's a very desperate and
very dramatic thing. Maybe it's a very rushed, frantic last
kiss before being taken out to the firing squad. Maybe they
[fans] wanted it to be a very tender, discovering moment,
but it wasn't. But that's Joe, he turns things over."

It was Sheridan's first time and the audience's first time,
but it is something Delenn has done many times before. "It
was great," says Mira Furlan. "I wish it was shot differently, though; I was a little bit disappointed by the way it was
shot. There were no eyes. Somehow the shadows [hid our
eyes] . . . Sometimes you have these visions of these scenes

and these moments, and then you see them and it's completely different."

So what is it like to kiss Bruce Boxleitner? "It's comfortable," she says. "Kissing is like anything else. It's a very technical thing in the end; you kind of sit there, they light you [and discuss], 'Shall we see this angle or that angle?' There's nothing romantic in it, it's part of the whole process, but people get excited by that as if it's a separate piece. We were actors, and then the kissing or the hugging or the lovemaking starts, and then we become completely different? No, we're the same people, professionals who do it. I've had some really bad experiences with other actors in my previous life, but this was so stressless, free of any kind of undercurrents. It was pure professionalism in the best sense."

When they are brought before Emperor Londo, we see that his behavior is being controlled by the keeper on his shoulder. This is not the first time we see a future in which Londo becomes emperor, but it is the first time it is more than a glimpse, and it gives actor Peter Jurasik more of a chance to play him as an old man. "It almost feels like you're playing a new character," he says. "It was fun to play the emperor again, the guy who gets to sit in the big seat and everybody bows to. That's always fun; we all want to play that. I got to interact with this little thing on my shoulder, the keeper. That was a wonderful element to add to the character."

Hidden in this scene are also partial explanations to other prophecies made in the past. In "Point of No Return," Lady Morella told Londo he had a chance to redeem himself if he did not kill the man who is already dead and, at the last, surrenders to his greatest fear. By setting Sheridan free, Londo follows the first of those directives (as, by this time, Sheridan will have already "died" on Z'ha'dum), and in asking G'Kar to kill him, he follows the second. The moment of Londo's death was something prophesied by a dream of his, first mentioned at the beginning of the first season in "Midnight on the Firing Line." At the time, it seemed to suggest that Londo would die as the result of his long-running feud with G'Kar. "War Without End" turns that around and shows instead that G'Kar kills him because of an understanding—not a rivalry—that has built up between them.

Andreas Katsulas, however, had trouble understanding exactly what was happening to his character of G'Kar in this flashforward. "I read it, and it was a jumble and a mess, and I told Joe, 'I think this stinks,' " says the actor. 'If I can't understand it reading it, how's the audience—who's seeing it go by like that [quickly]—going to understand it?' But I guess he's right, because the real avid fans who keep track of all of this understand all this flashforward in time and what it did to me. I follow the heart of G'Kar. The story and all its detail, I don't."

Andreas was not the only person to be confused by the complex nature of the story. It was densely packed with many interweaving plots, covering several time lines and possible futures. It was something that Mike Vejar had to get straight in his mind before directing the episodes. "I had more discussions about where we were in time during that episode than any I remember," he says. "It was very complex as far as what state people were in when they transferred from one dimension in time to the other. We tried to keep a different feel to each time dimension, with lighting and lenses, so that the audience would subliminally catch that we were in a different time frame."

The intricacies of time travel were so complex that Mike Vejar remembers getting it wrong in one sequence where Sheridan returns through time to Babylon 4. "I had Sheridan going to his knees, he fights and shakes and then goes out, which is incorrect for Joe's vision of how he was leaving at that particular moment. When he left Babylon 4, he was in agony, and I took him back the same way, which was incorrect for Joe. I think that was the one time in the show that I honestly didn't get where Joe was going with that, and he cut it in such a way that we never saw Sheridan go through those stages."

The episode was complex because it was moving in and out of time, telling Sinclair's story. Sheridan's story, and Babylon 4's story. Part of the difficulty was Babylon 4's story had already been partly told in the earlier episode "Babylon Squared." Events that happened then had to be repeated here, although the passage of almost two years since "Babylon Squared" necessitated some changes. "It was more logistical stuff than anything else," says Joe Straczynski. "The largest example is that in 'Babylon Squared' they mentioned that they found Zathras in the conference room. They were having a meeting and there was a flash of light and there was Zathras. What I had had in mind was that he was trying to get the equipment that he needs. He was in this one room and got caught in it. He tried to distract them and get out and, of course, was captured. When the time came to write that actual event in part two, I could do that scene and do it very easily, but the problem was that it would add about two and a half to three pages to a script that was already running long. I thought, 'I just can't do that.' It was him under the desk, waiting for people to get out, and they weren't leaving, and he finally had to do something. I just took it out of the conference room and put it into a hallway with some equipment. The same thing is happening, going to the equipment to see what he could find, but it wasn't in the conference room."

The conclusion of the episode is the conclusion of the Sinclair storyline. The man who was searching for a purpose in the first season finds his purpose at the end: to go into the past and become Valen. It is why Valen was always described as "Minbari not born of Minbari," how he was able to prophecy so much that happened in the future, and why Sinclair was not allowed to remember those twenty-four hours he spent with the Minbari Grey Council during the Battle of the Line. It explains why it is a "war without end," as the present war could be won only with a victory in the previous war. It is a loop of time that is turned by Sinclair. Valen creates the Minbari Grey Council; his soul then passes to the Human Sinclair, who then goes back in time to become Valen and repeat the process on and on forever.

"I was so glad we did it," concludes Bruce Boxleitner. "I was so glad we did it for Michael. It enabled him to come back and finish that line, that story, and what a way to finish. He goes away being God! If you're going to go out—go out that way!"

18
"Walkabout"

Cast

Captain John Sheridan ....Bruce Boxleitner
Commander Susan Ivanova ....Claudia Christian
Security Chief Michael Garibaldi ....Jerry Doyle
Ambassador Delenn ....Mira Furlan
Citizen G'Kar ....Andreas Katsulas
Ambassador Londo Mollari ....Peter Jurasik
Dr. Stephen Franklin ....Richard Biggs
Lennier ....Bill Mumy
Marcus Cole ....Jason Carter
Lyta Alexander ....Patricia Tallman
Vir Cotto ....Stephen Furst

Guest Stars

Cailyn ....Erica Gimpel
Dr. Hobbs ....Jennifer Balgobin
Na'Kal ....Robin Sachs

Lyta approaches the new Vorlon ambassador, a Vorlon who also calls himself "Kosh." It turns its headpiece, and an unseen force grips her throat. Lyta, almost unable to speak, apologizes for not being there when Kosh died. "There was no other?" the Vorlon intones. She says there was not, and reluctantly, he lets her go.

"I realized I had no idea who I was when I wasn't being a doctor," Franklin tells Garibaldi. "I think I was using the stims to avoid facing that. So now I have to fix it. The theory is, if you're separated from yourself, you start walking, and you keep walking until you meet yourself."

Franklin walks into a bar in Down Below where his attention is drawn to the singer on stage. He sits and watches intently. Her voice reaches out to him across the crowded room. *Afterward, the singer, Cailyn, takes him back to her quarters. She raises a glass to him, but instead of drinking, she peers through it, seeing Franklin's image reflected many times over by its pattern. "I'm looking at your soul," she tells him.*

Sheridan has decided to test their new weapon against the Shadows—telepathy. The White Star, *with telepath Lyta Alexander on board, emerges from hyperspace as a Shadow vessel finishes off the last of a fleet of alien ships. Lyta focuses her mind, and the Shadow vessel reacts, sensing her presence. It is cold, dark, foreboding. Lyta sinks to her knees, screaming as it pierces her mind. Sheridan pulls her up, and as their hands touch, the image of Kosh's death flashes through her mind. She stands and looks out at the Shadow vessel ahead of them, suddenly realizing what had happened. "They killed him," she says to herself, and turns to the Shadow vessel ahead of them. "Burn you bastard!" Lyta focuses, and the Shadow ship struggles against the power of her mind. Blood trickles from her eye as she holds the ship in her grip. The* White Star *fires a continuous beam of energy. The Shadow vessel buckles under its power, until the beam bursts through and the ship crumples like a dead spider.*

Franklin softly strokes Cailyn's back as they lie in bed together. It has been a long time since he has done something like this. He tells her he does not understand why someone of her talent is working in a Down Below bar and asks if he can help. The only thing she wants is a drug, metazine. He refuses, but when he wakes up the following morning, he finds her unconscious on the floor with a metazine bottle and his identicard in her hand.

Franklin looks at Cailyn as she lies in Medlab with a metazine drip. She was not addicted to the stuff; it was for her pain. She has terminal neural paralysis and, maybe, only seven months to live. Franklin says she could find better care on Earth, but she prefers to stay on Babylon 5, where her singing can reach the destitute of Down Below and really make a difference. "When they come and listen to me, for a moment you can see the hope in their eyes again," she says.

Lyta approaches the new Kosh. "Before, I told you I don't have a part of Kosh," she says, "but it may be that someone else does."

Later Franklin returns to the bar in Down Below to hear Cailyn sing again. He takes one last look before he walks away, passing by a patterned-glass partition that takes his image and reflects it many times over.

"Walkabout comes from the Australian aborigine culture," explains Joe Straczynski. "One thing I did for Franklin was to create a new Earth religion, which basically came up in the last one hundred fifty years or so. He's a Foundationist, and what the Foundationists have done is looked at all Human belief systems with the notion that there are many alien cultures and alien beliefs. Maybe what defines our religions and our beliefs is not denominations but what is the core of our beliefs. That makes us Human. I looked at a variety of Earth religions and went down to the core or the foundation of those beliefs and said, 'Let us incorporate this; let us draw upon the root of our beliefs rather than the schisms or the dogmas or the doctrines that were overlaid on top of that.' So they'd looked into everything from aboriginal beliefs to Muslim beliefs to Buddhism and sort of stitched together this quilt. Consequently, Franklin's beliefs have a wide number of traditions that spring into it, including the aborigine notion."

"I think the doctor's trying to reach out," says Franklin actor Richard Biggs. "He's desperately trying to balance his life and trying to evolve into something else. I think it's a desperate move. You see someone who usually thinks things out; he plans, he schedules. In this episode, you see someone making spur-of-the-moment decisions, instinctual. He meets this woman, he likes this woman, he sleeps with this woman. That's not the doctor. That is somebody trying to step out of his skin because he knows he has a problem."

Franklin gets involved with Cailyn, the singer from Down Below, as part of his journey to rediscover himself. He told

Sheridan when he resigned from Medlab that he had not just sat and listened to music for a long time. Now he does that and more, becoming absorbed by the music and the singer.

The lyrics of the songs that Cailyn sings were written by Joe Straczynski and, in some ways, reflect on Babylon 5's situation. "Mainly in terms of tonality," says Joe. "A lot of the show is mood stuff, and a lot of that sets the mood for what is in the story and for what Franklin and the others are going through. I knew I wanted to get Franklin involved with a singer in Down Below, and when the time came to write that episode, I thought, 'We're going to need some songs here, and we'll just go to Christopher [Franke, the show's composer] to get a couple of songs written.' Then I thought, 'Wait a minute, I've written songs before—I *like* doing it—I might as well take a shot at it. If they're crummy, Chris will tell me and scrap it and we'll have him do it.' So I wrote the two songs, and oddly enough, they both took me about an hour each, which is not that long. Chris read them, thought they were just fine, did the music for them, and dropped them in."

The episode tells Cailyn's story—her terminal illness, her decision to sing in Down Below and live for the moment—but it is really about Franklin and how his relationship with the singer reflects back on him. A nice touch is created in the way Franklin's metaphor of having lost part of himself is echoed in the multiple images of him seen through Cailyn's liquor glass. "Joe was real specific with the looking through the glass and the multiple images of Franklin," says director Kevin Cremin. "The minute I read that in the script, I said, 'Guys, let's start going around finding glasses.' We went through about twenty-five to thirty glasses to find the right one, but we did it in preproduction so I wasn't too nervous. If we'd done it on the set, while the whole crew was standing around—*then* I would have been nervous!"

The theme of "walkabout" is introduced at the beginning of the episode, when Sheridan takes a walk on the outside of the station and watches the new Vorlon ambassador's ship arrive. The new Vorlon brings a much darker tone with him to *Babylon 5*. Like the first ambassador, he calls himself

Kosh, but there is a sense in which this Vorlon is very different from his predecessor. "He is and he isn't," says Joe. "By the end of his period on Babylon 5, the original Kosh had become almost a Vorlon chatterbox by their standards. This one was right back to the original version of 'I only say one or two words, and then I walk out the door.' Certainly his first scene with Lyta, where he basically grabs her by the throat and demands to know what happened, sets up that this is not the same friendly Vorlon we have seen before. This is a dark Vorlon. In my head, this was a more military version, where the original Kosh was more of a diplomat. He is more of a soldier who wants to know what's going on and why things aren't proceeding to plan."

Lyta is obviously loyal to the new Vorlon, but she also has an affinity to the Humans on Babylon 5. It is a split loyalty that is to become more pronounced in the fourth season, but here she is putting herself on the line for the Humans, using her telepathic powers against the Shadows. "I thought that was pretty neat because it gave Lyta a future: now Lyta has a purpose, she can fight the Shadows, she can be useful," says actress Patricia Tallman. "So she's not just a Vorlon disciple; she really has a job that she can do."

Because Lyta fights the Shadow vessel with her mind, the onus was really on the actress and the computer graphics to dramatize the conflict for the audience. "I'm acting with a blue screen," says Pat Tallman. "And they're telling me what's happening—'You're concentrating so hard, you bleed from your eye'—and there's arguments about where the blood should come from, whether it's from the inside or the outside. I said it should come from the inside, but they put it on the outside—I still don't like how that looks. They're going, 'Now the Shadow ship shoots back, and you need to react to it,' and I do what I think looks right, but the director's saying, 'Well, that doesn't look right. I want to try something else.' We're trying so hard to make it look real, and I'm acting in my own head, and I've got to trust the director to tell me what works or not."

Kevin Cremin had discussed these scenes with Joe Straczynski and had a clear idea of how he was going to direct them—until he spoke to Pat Tallman. "She's quite a fascinating actress," he says. "She had been talking to Joe about the character and about playing those scenes, and when she came down on the set, we had a couple of discussions about a few things. She was so convincing in the way that she was posing these questions to me that, after talking to her, I started to think, 'My God, Joe has changed his mind since I talked to him,' or 'Maybe he's looking at alternate ways of doing this.' So I shot a couple of sequences a couple of different ways because Pat Tallman had brought up what I thought was a valid point, and I didn't have a real good answer for her at the time."

The telepathy experiment works, but the *White Star* would probably have been destroyed by other Shadow vessels if G'Kar had not arrived with a fleet of ships. The War Council's original plan was for a Narn captain to provide military backup for the *White Star*, but he refused. It may have taken Garibaldi to nudge G'Kar in the right direction, but he accepted it as his responsibility to help. "Here's a good example of the gap between what G'Kar's feeling and the rest of the Narn mentality, which hasn't yet come to the consciousness," says Andreas Katsulas, who plays G'Kar. "G'Kar sees things very clearly, but it's, 'How do I convince the captain?' He can understand the captain can't do anything about it, but I can take my personal fighter and I can persuade others. He's working for the good and not letting anything become an obstacle."

19
"Grey 17 Is Missing"

Cast

Captain John Sheridan ....Bruce Boxleitner
Commander Susan Ivanova ....Claudia Christian
Security Chief Michael Garibaldi ....Jerry Doyle
Ambassador Delenn ....Mira Furlan
Citizen G'Kar ....Andreas Katsulas
Ambassador Londo Mollari ....Peter Jurasik
Dr. Stephen Franklin ....Richard Biggs
Lennier ....Bill Mumy
Marcus Cole ....Jason Carter
Lyta Alexander ....Patricia Tallman
Vir Cotto ....Stephen Furst

Guest Stars

First Man ....Eamonn Roache
Maintenance Worker ....Thom Berry
Jeremiah ....Robert Englund
Rathenn ....Time Winters
Shai Alyt Neroon ....John Vickery
Supervisor ....Katherine Moffat

*Delenn looks through Sinclair's possessions that were
left on Minbar. An Earth Alliance insignia, his Medal of
Valor from the Battle of the Line, and a Ranger brooch.
Now that he is gone, a new leader is needed for the
Rangers. Delenn is taken aback to hear that the name
suggested is her own.*

*Neroon—the warrior caste Minbari who replaced
Delenn on the Grey Council—finds Delenn and tells her
to hand over control of the Rangers to the warrior caste.
"I am sworn to stop you, Delenn. By any and all means
necessary."*

Marcus stands before Neroon and, with a flick of his

wrist, extends his fighting pike, ready to fight to protect Delenn. "The only way you will get to her is through me," says Marcus. "I invoke denn-shah." A fight to the death.

Marcus strikes, his pike clanging against Neroon's pike as the Minbari blocks him. Neroon swipes at Marcus and hits him in the face, drawing blood. Marcus strikes back, grazing Neroon's cheek. Neroon brings his pike down hard on Marcus's side, breaking two of his ribs and sending him spinning into the wall and to the ground. Neroon stands over Marcus, his pike poised, ready for the deathblow. But first he asks him why. "For her," says Marcus. "We live for The One, we die for The One."

Zack walks in on Garibaldi as he is cleaning an antique "slug-thrower" gun that used to belong to his grandmother. Zack explains that a maintenance man has gone missing in Grey Sector. Garibaldi decides to check it out. "I like mysteries," he says, pocketing the bullets and putting his gun away.

Maintenance says they've checked out all twenty-nine levels of Grey Sector and found no trace of the missing man. Garibaldi is suspicious. There should be thirty levels in Grey Sector. He takes the transport tube, counting the three seconds it takes to get to each floor, until he gets to Grey 17. Six seconds. He tries it again and, after three seconds, calls an emergency stop. He pries apart the doors and steps into a darkened corridor strewn with rubbish—the real Grey 17.

Jeremiah welcomes Garibaldi to Grey 17, which he, and the others who live there, have annexed from the rest of the station in their search for purity. "The only way out is to find purity in purpose, thought, or belief," says Jeremiah. "That is the door of the mind, the way out. But there must be a way out for the body." A hideous roar echoes down the corridor, and Garibaldi realizes the "way out" Jeremiah speaks of is death.

The roar belongs to a Zarg, the most dangerous alien in the sector. Garibaldi rips a steam pipe off the wall and *fashions a gun barrel from a piece of metal tubing on the floor. The Zarg emerges from the darkness, and Garibaldi drops the bullets from his pocket into the pipe. The steam ignites the gunpowder, and the bullets fly wildly. Two of them strike the Zarg in the chest, and Garibaldi and Jeremiah head out past its body.*

Neroon approaches Delenn at the ceremony that marks her appointment as Ranger One. He drops his bloody Minbari fighting pike to the floor. "They would not die for me, but they would die for you," he says, bowing his head.

Marcus lies in Medlab, badly beaten, but alive.

"The death was mine," Neroon tells him. "Strange that a Human in his last moments should be more of a Minbari than I."

"Grey 17 Is Missing" is generally regarded as the weakest episode of the third season. Joe Straczynski agrees that, while most of his script works well on screen, it is ultimately let down by the Zarg, which is clearly a man in a rubber suit. "I should have learned my lesson about rubber-suit monsters," he says. "I learned it with the Zarg, finally."

The idea that a whole section of Babylon 5 could have "disappeared" without anyone really noticing is an intriguing one. The idea of discovering a lost world is something that has long fascinated people, from the Greek myth of Atlantis to modern stories of parallel dimensions. What Garibaldi finds in the "missing" Grey 17 is a fervent group of people in search of perfection. Their leader, Jeremiah, believes that people have been created by the universe in an attempt to understand itself. Molecules and atoms released by the stars are recycled into people, who, when they die, are themselves recycled in an attempt to purify and eventually find perfection. Jeremiah mentions that his beliefs relate to those of the Minbari, and in fact, they echo Delenn's sentiments in "A Distant Star," where she described people as "starstuff." Indeed, her phrase, "We are the universe made manifest," is something that Jeremiah repeats here. But somehow those ideas do not come alive on camera. "The

Jeremiah thread was one of those things that looks great on paper," says Joe. "I'm happy with all the other stuff in the episode, but the Jeremiah thread didn't come off as it should've."

Part of the problem is that these ideas are expressed entirely in dialogue. Jeremiah tells Garibaldi, rather than shows him, about his philosophy. It does not help that Garibaldi has no interest in what Jeremiah is preaching; all he wants to do is find a way out. If Garibaldi could have been in some way convinced, it might have drawn the audience into considering Jeremiah's ideas. Had that been achieved, it would have demonstrated the final irony of Jeremiah's little cult, that the only way to find perfection in life is through death.

The episode was a chance to spotlight Garibaldi. In the first and second seasons, episodes like "Survivors," "The Long Dark," and "Hunter, Prey" had highlighted his character, but the momentous events of the third season had not allowed the security chief to appear in many stories of this nature. "Grey 17 Is Missing" redresses that balance somewhat, but Jerry Doyle feels that the material was not as inspired as some of the other scripts he has worked with on *Babylon 5*. "I'm not big on killing monsters," says the actor. "I'm big on talking to people. I'm big on relationships stuff, character relationships stuff. Killing monsters has got its place, but it's not one of my favorites."

The title "Grey 17 Is Missing" disguises the other major plotline in the episode, which is more significant in terms of the overall arc. This story sees Delenn ascend to the position of Entil-Zah, The One who commands the Rangers. It works much better as it uses this event to bring out the conflicts and loyalties of the characters. Neroon's opposition to Delenn leading what is, in effect, a military outfit highlights the rift between the Minbari religious and warrior castes. He accuses her of craving power, but in reality, it is a power she shirks away from. She did not automatically see herself as the next Ranger One after Sinclair and had to be persuaded to take up that position. Even when she does, she does not fully realize what it means to be Entil-Zah. Lennier has to point out to her that she is now so important to the Rangers that they are willing to die for her. "She hated that, and she was totally opposed to that," says actress Mira Furlan. "She became aware of her power, and it frightened her. There was nothing good in that sentence, that thought, 'People are dying for me.' She's a different kind of being, so that is a sentence filled with anxiety."

The fact that Lennier is the one who demonstrates this to Delenn is an indication of the character's development. He was very naive when he arrived on the station, not even able to look her in the eye. Now he has the strength of character to go against her wishes, enlisting Marcus's help to stop Neroon. "That was a good show for Lennier," says actor Bill Mumy. "On the subtle level, when the attention is on Lennier, you will notice that he has absorbed a lot of responsibility and is quite comfortable directing others and getting things done, standing there and taking care of business. Then, of course, in the bigger, more obvious storyline, he has basically manipulated Marcus into a near-death situation. Lennier carries around some guilt for that, regardless of the fact that it ended without Marcus's death."

The fight sequence between Marcus and Neroon is one of the major one-on-one fights of the season and is spread across several scenes. These two are well-matched warriors, fighting to the death, but in the end, it is experience that wins out over youth and determination. "The thing I liked about that particularly was it was focused intent," says Marcus actor Jason Carter. "Most of the fights that you see Marcus in are with fairly random unpleasant individuals that have to be taken care of. Personality doesn't particularly become involved. When you're dealing one-on-one with someone who is famed for being such a great fighter, you know you're outclassed, and it's that focus—it's very hard not to know you're going to lose, there's just a determination. That's where Marcus's honor comes in, determination to fulfill a particular role. If his role in that moment is to die in order that Delenn will live, then—okay, he'll do his damnedest not to die—but he'll try and fulfill that obligation."

This fight sequence, like most that appear in *Babylon 5*,

was filmed using a combination of stunt artists and actors. "My arrogance in being a Brit is I want to bloody do the whole fight," says Jason, "but you're fighting the precedents of the insurance company and also the precedents of the number of other actors who have actually managed to injure themselves. The fact that I don't injure myself, or haven't ever, doesn't come into it. It's a rule, a bureaucratic rule. But Kerry [Rossall, the stunt coordinator] will direct the fight, and I will pay as much attention to it as I can and practice it and do it alongside. Then they'll shoot it with the stunt guys, and then they'll shoot it with me. The only thing is if there's time for me to do the whole sequence. That's a personal frustration because I like to do the whole thing, arrogant bastard that I am!"

This episode was directed by John C. Flinn III who, as the show's resident director of photography, filmed much of the fight by putting the camera on his shoulder and getting in the fray with the actors. "He's egging me on to come at him, and I'm whacking the camera!" says Jason. "So, there I am, hitting the camera with my pike, and everyone else looks shocked. They don't know that John's behind the camera going, 'Go on, go on,' growling at me."

"That was brutal," says John Flinn. "I got my chest hit by that baton, I got hit in the stomach, I got hit in the knees, I got hit in the head, but we went for it. It was a tough fight, it was a brutal fight, but that's what they called for. When we got done with that day I felt that I had been in a total real brawl. I get so excited doing it that I don't care."

The fight proves to Neroon that Delenn is the right one to lead the Rangers. She may not have the military training that he has had, but she is a spiritual leader who can inspire them to such an extent that they are willing to die for her. His reconciliation with Marcus and with Delenn overcomes the immediate problem, but it does not resolve the problem of the disbanded Grey Council. That, we are reminded by this episode, is an issue that has not been put to rest and one that is certain to resurface before the great saga is over.

20
"And the Rock Cried Out, 'No Hiding Place' "

Cast

Captain John Sheridan	Bruce Boxleitner
Commander Susan Ivanova	Claudia Christian
Security Chief Michael Garibaldi	Jerry Doyle
Ambassador Delenn	Mira Furlan
Citizen G'Kar	Andreas Katsulas
Ambassador Londo Mollari	Peter Jurasik
Dr. Stephen Franklin	Richard Biggs
Lennier	Bill Mumy
Marcus Cole	Jason Carter
Lyta Alexander	Patricia Tallman
Vir Cotto	Stephen Furst

Guest Stars

Lord Refa	William Forward
Brother Theo	Louis Turenne
Reverend Will Dexter	Men Winkler

Londo has decided that it is time to deal with G'Kar. "I want you to go to G'Kar and tell him that Na'Toth is alive," Londo tells Vir. "Knowing G'Kar, once he hears this, he'll return to Narn at once."

Vir performs his duty but is captured by agents of Lord Refa and thrown into a locked, darkened room. A single light is turned on, illuminating Refa. "You will tell me what Londo is planning, or you will not leave this room alive," says Refa, calling forward a telepath. The telepath stares into Vir's mind and, as he struggles against the inevitable, pulls every detail of Londo's conversation from him.

*A group of religious leaders are on Babylon 5,
ostensibly to provide guidance and comfort to those on
board but covertly to bring news of the situation back
on Earth. One of them, Reverend Will Dexter, notices
Sheridan's tiredness and calls on him late at night when
he is wading through a pile of mundane station reports.
He says that during the Earth-Minbari War, he learned
to tell the good officers from the bad officers. "The bad
ones were loaded down with this sense of terrible
responsibility," he says, and tells him he ought to share
some of his responsibility with Delenn.*

*Back in the war room, Sheridan takes another look at
the map of apparently random Shadow attacks, this time
with Delenn at his side. He suddenly notices something
that he had not seen before. The Shadows have not
attacked the center of the galaxy. It would seem they are
driving refugees into the quiet zone, so as to make one
major, devastating strike.*

*Delenn insists that Sheridan attend Reverend Dexter's
service in the station chapel. Meanwhile, G'Kar has
arrived on Narn and has been met by Lord Refa. G'Kar
flicks a switch on a small holographic projector he has in
his hand, and the image of Londo appears before them.
"You have taken from me that which I loved, Refa,"
Londo's hologram says. "It is not enough for me simply
to kill you. Through your death here, I will discredit
your house and all opposition in the royal court. Good-
bye, Refa."*

*G'Kar strokes his finger across Refa's throat. "Leave
his face and head intact," he says to the group of
Narns who are with him. "They will need it for
identification." Panic spreads across Refa's face, and
he turns and runs.*

*The joyous sound of gospel singing fills the chapel on
Babylon 5—"The rock cried out, 'No hiding place, no
hiding place down here . . .' "—as the Narns pursue
Refa through the dark underground tunnels of Narn.
Four Narns block his path. He turns back, desperately*

*looking for an escape route. "They'll be running, trying
to find a hiding place . . ." He is blocked on all sides by
Narns and unyielding rock. "No hiding place down
here." They throw him against the wall, and the crowd
fights to tear his body apart.*

*Londo gives the data crystal found on Refa's body
to Centauri minister Virini. It shows that Refa was
helping the Narn resistance in order to get power for
himself in the royal court. It angers Vir to realize
Londo lied to him in order to lure Refa into G'Kar's
hands.*

Delenn takes Sheridan on a journey in the White Star
*to where a fleet of a hundred White Star ships are
waiting for him. He looks at the ships in wonder, then
back at her. They draw closer, looking into each other's
eyes, and kiss. A long, easy, intense kiss.*

"No one is safe," is Joe Straczynski's philosophy when it comes to characters. "Any character can drop down a hole at a moment's notice, which is great for the audience because then the jeopardy becomes real. In the average show you know the character will escape at the end. Here you don't know that."

"And the Rock Cried Out, 'No Hiding Place' " saw the demise of Refa, the Centauri whose ambitions are as great as Londo's but whose schemings, in the end, are not quite a match for his adversary's. William Forward's Refa began as just another guest Centauri but soon became a key link between Londo and Centauri Prime. Over nearly two years, he turned from being Londo's ally into being the Shadows' ally and Londo's enemy. "I have to mention how wonderful Bill Forward was," says fellow actor Peter Jurasik. "Such a good fun actor. He took this little character that showed up and just gave himself up to it. He was so slimy as Refa, there was something so wonderful. To me, he always keyed on the lean and hungry of Cassius in *Julius Caesar* that Shakespeare refers to. No matter where Bill was, you felt he was lurking as Refa. It always felt like he was fifteen feet away, staring at you. That was the end of his role with us, but he was a terrific actor."

Refa had become so entwined with Londo and the conspiracies on Centauri Prime that many people were sad to see him go. That fact, of course, merely added to the impact of his death, and Joe Straczynski makes no apologies for killing him off. "I was more interested in the character of Londo and dropping him further down the pit than I was in preserving Refa," he says. "Thus, I thought, what if I drop Refa? What if I just kill him? How would it effect Londo? How would it effect G'Kar? Oddly, it would put Londo and G'Kar on the same side."

The maneuvering that is needed to get G'Kar to work for Londo is beautifully orchestrated. The audience is brought to believe that G'Kar is being led to his death on Narn, when, in reality, it is Refa who is going to die. It is an interesting and surprising twist to see these two great enemies, Londo and G'Kar, working with each other, and adds further complexities to their already complex relationship. This plot thread also conspires to bring G'Kar to Narn, where he sees the devastation of his home planet with his own eyes for the first time. "Seeing your homeworld, which was once green with squirrels running up the trees, is now suddenly windblown and desolate," says Andreas Katsulas, who plays G'Kar, "is especially poignant for him, because he hasn't been there to suffer along with other people every bomb that hit and every stone that was hurled; he was safely away in his nice comfortable apartment on Babylon 5."

Londo cannot be at Refa's execution because he would be implicated, but we are not robbed of a last showdown between these two. Londo gets to say his piece to Refa by way of a holographic message. The effect works well on screen, but it was complicated to film because Londo had to be filmed separately from the other characters and later placed into the scene by computer. "You have to rehearse it over and over again, more so than any other type of scene," says director David Eagle. "You've got to shoot everybody except Londo in the scene. So he's doing his lines literally a few feet off stage, and everybody is looking to where they've seen him go in rehearsal. Then we take them out and put just him in and he walks around and does his thing. Then we take him and everybody out and just shoot a few seconds of the empty set. By the time we'd done all that for one scene, four hours has passed. It's complicated, and you just have to make sure that you get it right, and I think we did. I purposely did not want him always directly looking at Refa because this was just a hologram, he's not actually there."

"That's hard stuff to do," says Andreas, "especially for me, who loves to be emotional and really get into it, suddenly acting with absolutely nothing. When the hologram went through me I had to shiver. I didn't know how to act it. It's all tricky stuff. Peter comes in, and he walks through it, so you have a sense of where he went. You rehearse it in that way, so you remember he walked there and stood next to so-and-so, but then you're working from memory and you're watching the ghost of Peter do this. High tech."

Refa's death scenes, running away in panic with the Narns closing in on him, were juxtaposed quite deliberately with the gospel singing back on Babylon 5. "It's a very creepy and subversive thing to do, to juxtapose those two images," says Joe Straczynski. "I love, once and so often, to get a little bit on the subversive side. The song is happy and upbeat, and everyone is laughing and clapping, and this guy is being killed. You're cutting back and forth. Emotionally the audience is horrified he is being killed, [while at the same time knowing] this is the bad guy, so emotionally you don't know which way to cut. All you can do is sit there with your jaw open and watch it happening. We made it even creepier by taking the last fifteen seconds of the music and distorting it slightly so it's got a hollow echo to it, which made that wonderful smiling music sound suddenly rather ominous. I love messing with an audience. If I've got the audience where they just don't know where to go emotionally, that, to me, is a perfect moment."

The small subplot running throughout the episode, coinciding with the religious leaders' visit, concerns Sheridan and Delenn's relationship. She is seen nagging him on several occasions, almost like they are already married. During these scenes, Delenn talks about her confusion over the language. She doesn't understand the word "cranky," so she looks it up to find it means "grouchy," then has to look up "grouchy," only to find it means "crotchety." It has certain parallels to Mira Furlan who, as a Yugoslavian living in an English-speaking country, always has a dictionary in her bag. "I constantly write words down to look them up," she says. "That's one of the only advantages, one of the rare advantages of speaking a foreign language; you always feel that you're advancing, you're improving, because you're always learning new words—which just means you're in big trouble because your vocabulary is so small. But for me it's fun because I'm interested in languages, and it fills me with joy when I learn some new fun word or expression. But yeah, I'm looking up words all the time."

These fun, light scenes culminate in Sheridan and Delenn's first kiss in the present. After so much teasing, they finally reveal their love for each other in the way everyone has been waiting for. "Everybody was aware—Bruce and Mira in particular—that this was the first time these two characters really kissed," says director David Eagle. "We talked about how to do it and the importance of this particular first kiss, and I think they really came through and made it look like that."

"That was the first deep kiss?" says Bruce. "I've kissed her so many times since then I can't remember! Most of the time, we have to do it in such a technical way that it seems very technical while we're doing it. We are both adult people; we know how to kiss. Mira and I get on terrifically; we don't have any real shyness about it. They're always so technical. I always complain, it's 'Don't move this, you're causing a shadow, now act like you're totally in love and free with each other.' So I'm always more surprised when I see the scenes than when we've done them."

When they eventually kiss, it is against the backdrop of a fleet of White Stars, and that is the image the audience is left with at the end of the episode. An image of two people finding out about each other, learning to love each other, against the backdrop of war.

21
"Shadow Dancing"

Cast

Captain John Sheridan ....Bruce Boxleitner
Commander Susan Ivanova ....Claudia Christian
Security Chief Michael Garibaldi ....Jerry Doyle
Ambassador Delenn ....Mira Furlan
Citizen G'Kar ....Andreas Katsulas
Ambassador Londo Mollari ....Peter Jurasik
Dr. Stephen Franklin ....Richard Biggs
Lennier ....Bill Mumy
Marcus Cole ....Jason Carter
Lyta Alexander ....Patricia Tallman
Vir Cotto ....Stephen Furst

Guest Stars

Drazi Ambassador ....Mark Hendrickson
Brakiri ....Jonathan Chapman
Corwin ....Joshua Cox
Barbara ....Shirley Prestia
Husband ....Doug Cox
Thug No. 1 ....Nicholas Ross Olson
Thug No. 2 ....John Grantham
Man ....J. Gordon Noice
Anna Sheridan ....Melissa Gilbert

Delenn appeals to the League of Non-Aligned Worlds to take a stand against the Shadows in what she expects will be their biggest attack yet. They agree to send as many ships as they can spare.

Franklin turns the corner in a dismal part of Brown Sector to see two thugs beating up a drug dealer. "Hey! Leave him alone!" he calls. One of the men turns on Franklin and slams him up against the wall. He pulls out a knife and rams it hard into Franklin's stomach.

*Franklin cries out and sinks to the floor, as they run off
leaving him to bleed to death.*

*A jump point opens, and hundreds and hundreds of
Minbari, Drazi, and other League ships spill out into the
area the Shadows have chosen as their next
battleground. Sheridan and Delenn stand in the viewing
chamber on the Minbari war cruiser at the head of the
fleet. The walls and floor seem to ripple and become
transparent, as if they were standing with nothing but
space between them and the two fleets of ships. "Break
and attack," orders Sheridan, and the fleet advances,
firing at the Shadows as telepaths reach out with their
minds to slow the enemy down.*

*Franklin clutches his stomach, blood seeping through
his fingers. He calls weakly for help, but there is no one
around to hear him. "Always trying to be the hero,"
says a voice. "Never stopping to think first." Franklin
looks up and sees—inexplicably—himself, in uniform,
looking down at him. "All your life, you've run away,"
he says disapprovingly. "Take responsibility for yourself.
Don't just walk away because it's easier."*

*Beams of energy crisscross through space as the
Shadow and the League ships strike at each other.
Explosions blaze like fireworks in a night sky, as ships
are destroyed and their component pieces fly out in all
directions. A Drazi Sunhawk fires a continuous burst at
a Shadow vessel, which glows with the energy and
squirms to get free, until a second ship adds its firepower
to the first, and the Shadow vessel explodes. Elsewhere,
a Shadow vessel strikes at a Minbari war cruiser, ripping
it in two.*

*Franklin stares down disapprovingly at his bleeding
other self. "I want . . ." begins the injured Franklin.
"What do you want?" goads his other self. "I want . . .
to do it all again . . ." he replies, and clasps at rungs on
the wall with bloody hands, pulling himself to his feet.*

*Shadow vessels retreat from the battle, shimmering
away into hyperspace, leaving behind many of their own*

disabled, crumpled, and broken ships. Sheridan and Delenn stand in the viewing chamber, looking at the scene of their victory. Pieces of broken League ships tumble past. Sheridan holds Delenn close, but he cannot take his eyes off the destroyed ships that mark the terrible price they've paid for victory.

Franklin, staggering, leaving his other self behind, moves step by painful step through Brown Sector until he finds people. "I want to do it all over again," he gasps as he collapses in the middle of the crowded marketplace.

Sheridan lies in bed, the calmness of sleep reflected on his face. Delenn watches him for a moment, as part of the Minbari tradition for two people who are close. Then she moves over to the table and picks up a snow globe that Sheridan keeps there. She looks up as she hears the door open. "Hello," says the woman standing in the doorway. "I'm Anna Sheridan. John's wife." The globe slips from Delenn's fingers and smashes to the floor.

The latter half of the third season was all leading up to this episode: the first head-on confrontation with the Shadows. Once Babylon 5 had broken away from Earth, events focused on its next major fight. From the discovery that telepaths could be used as a weapon, in "Ship of Tears," to the deployment of a fleet of White Stars, in "And the Rock Cried Out, 'No Hiding Place,' " each episode brought the characters a step closer to the inevitable. And the inevitable confrontation was no disappointment, utilizing some of the most intense CGI sequences of the whole series. Their impact was strengthened by putting Sheridan and Delenn in the center of it, with the spectacle of the battle seen all around them, as it was for the Minbari Grey Council in flashbacks to the Battle of the Line.

"I liked the way it looked; it looked really great," says Mira Furlan, who plays Delenn. "It was edited wonderfully. But it was horrible to shoot because you don't know anything; you're just in the dark, you feel so false. Talk about falseness. 'Here they are, they're coming.' Nobody can enjoy that. I enjoy a real relationship, real stuff, this 'ball,' I throw it to you, you throw it to me. But when you are playing without anything, you have no idea what you're doing, you're just a toy and the editor or the director is the one who actually calls the shots. He's the master, you're a small part of it."

"That was hard to do," adds Sheridan actor Bruce Boxleitner. "In fact, I had to go in and do some postproduction on that sound-wise. I had a hard time seeing all this; I thought we were so far removed from it. It was difficult, so I had to go in there and redub some of my dialogue so it was a little stronger, a little more forceful. Also, I think I was coming down with something. I was very tired, I had to come in and put a little more energy into it."

The buildup to the battle comes from sending Ivanova and Marcus onto the battlefield, as it were, to scout for the Shadow fleet. We are told it is a mission from which they have only a fifty-fifty chance of coming back alive. When they engage the Shadow scout ship, it is merely the beginning of their being put in direct danger. Once again, it is a battle constructed mostly in the computer, with the actors contributing just a small part to the whole.

"You're responding to exteriors that you don't know," says Marcus actor Jason Carter. "You just have to go for it and turn the volume up on the reactions. What you haven't got when you're doing it—the floor isn't shaking, and there isn't an incredible noise, and there isn't this powerful battle happening, with all the sound effects and all of that stuff that goes on. It's also an edit job: if you edit from a big shock that you've seen outside in CGI to everyone falling over and cut straight out of it, it doesn't matter, because you're moving at high speed and you're connecting the two images in the brain. "Oh look, the ship shook, and there they are falling over. That makes sense." So the audience does the work and fills in the blanks, which is good, otherwise we'd all get very, very hurt!"

"It's quite tedious in a way, because you have about seven pages of dialogue and they break it into individual lines," adds Claudia Christian, who plays Ivanova. "So it's like, 'Fire away.' And you do that again, 'Fire away' and cut. "You relight, and the next scene is 'Straight ahead,' or whatever. Then you wait another hour, and you get to say, 'Fluck shawl!' It's like all day long you're throwing one-liners out, and it gets kind of boring after a while—but hey, it's a job!"

The subplot of the episode is the resolution to Franklin's walkabout. He finally does meet himself and get to work out some of the things that made him quit his job in Medlab. There has been some debate over whether it was appropriate to tell his individual story while the rest of the galaxy was fighting for its future. "My sense is once you've seen one battle you've seen them all," says Joe Straczynski. "Once you've seen ships blow up, you've seen ships blow up, and there is nothing fundamentally new you can do with that. There are some folks who only want to see battle sequences. I've seen kinds of folks who, because there wasn't a battle sequence in an episode, figured nothing happened in the episode, and those are, to my mind, propeller-heads. I'm here for the human drama, and that intercutting is there to remind you: yeah, you've got this huge canvas and things blowing up and big battles, but what is that battle about? It is about the right of individuals to stand up and decide for themselves what they want to do, which is exactly what Franklin is doing. That is the obligation we have every day, to decide what we want, how we live our lives, and how we achieve meaning. We don't always have a chance to do that in battle. You do it in the office, you do it with your family, you do it in the courtroom, you do it in the day-to-day ethical way you live your life. So what Franklin was enduring was absolutely at the heart and core of what the battle was about. Thematically, one reflects the other and reminds you that the human being singular is where our concern really has to be."

Franklin's metaphor of looking for the other part of himself by walking through the station seems to come to life as he lies bleeding to death in Down Below. Actor Richard Biggs had to play against himself in these scenes, playing Franklin #1, then changing costume and positions to play

Franklin #2. "You've got another stand-in actor that you're playing with, so it was just like any other scene," he says. "I really tried not to think, 'Oh, this actor's really not going to be there.' I really tried to play to that particular actor, so that each time you see me, whether it's meeting myself or I'm being stabbed, I'm playing off of something. I really tried to show two different characters. I don't think that Franklin is a relaxed character; I think he's on guard all the time. But the Franklin inside his head is much more relaxed, he has much more expression, he is more able to express how he feels, and I tried to give that fluid type of performance."

Franklin's walkabout is a way for him to answer two questions that run through much of the show: "Who are you?" and "What do you want?" The conversation he has with himself helps to define the man he is and make him realize that what he wants is to do it all again. Only then does he make the effort to crawl back to the world he left.

The Minbari ritual in which the female watches the male sleep is somewhat a reflection of that. Like the way Franklin went on walkabout to find his true self, Delenn watches Sheridan sleep to see the face of the real man. "It's interesting," reflects Mira Furlan. "What kind of energy, what kind of vibes come out of you while you're sleeping. The idea's obviously to see what's happening when you lose control over your actions and your appearances. She's talking about how we all put masks on and how they fall when we sleep. What's underneath? What did she see? You can be in touch with his soul in a more direct way. That's why people who love each other sleep together, I guess."

Many viewers realized that this was, in fact, the second time Delenn had watched Sheridan sleep. She had also done so on the *White Star* in "Messages from Earth." That means that after this night, there is only one more to go before the ritual is concluded. But what promised to be a quiet and reflective moment after the battle is shattered when a figure from the past walks through the door, and the stage is set for the season's finale.

22
"Z'ha'dum"

Cast

Captain John Sheridan	Bruce Boxleitner
Commander Susan Ivanova	Claudia Christian
Security Chief Michael Garibaldi	Jerry Doyle
Ambassador Delenn	Mira Furlan
Citizen G'Kar	Andreas Katsulas
Ambassador Londo Mollari	Peter Jurasik
Dr. Stephen Franklin	Richard Biggs
Lennier	Bill Mumy
Marcus Cole	Jason Carter
Lyta Alexander	Patricia Tallman
Vir Cotto	Stephen Furst

Guest Stars

Anna Sheridan	Melissa Gilbert
Justin	Jeff Corey
Morden	Ed Wasser
Corwin	Joshua Cox

Sheridan grabs Delenn by the shoulders and pulls her around to face him. "You gave me every reason to believe she was dead! Now how could you do that when you didn't know for sure?" Delenn turns away from him. She cannot explain why his wife has returned from the Shadows' homeworld, Z'ha'dum.

G'Kar shows Ivanova a new range of weapons just delivered to Babylon 5; mines that can deliver a thermonuclear blast of up to six hundred megatons. "The captain will be very happy about this," says Ivanova.

Sheridan lays Anna's medical report to one side and turns to look at her. "You've been on Z'ha'dum all these years? Doing what?" She refuses to tell him, not while they are on Babylon 5. She wants him to go to Z'ha'dum to learn the Shadows' side of the story. He nods. "I'll go," he says. She smiles and throws her arms around him, but as he holds her, his troubled eyes move across to the medical report. It shows that marks on her neck match those on Human telepaths adapted to function inside Shadow ships.

Sheridan and Anna take the White Star, and then go by shuttle down to Z'ha'dum. There he is welcomed by Justin, "a sort of middleman," and Morden. Justin explains that the Shadows are promoting wars because they believe in strength through conflict. "Look at the long history of Human struggle," says Morden. "We never would have come this far if we hadn't been at each other's throats, evolving our way up inch by inch."

C & C detects a disturbance around Babylon 5. Dozens of Shadow vessels shimmer into existence and surround the station.

Anna tells Sheridan that the wars have become unbalanced because the Vorlons have enlisted the help of other races. "They've manipulated us so we'd respond to them favorably," says Morden. "They've even interfered at the genetic level. Why do you think certifiable telepaths came out of nowhere a hundred years ago?"

Justin wants Sheridan to work with them, but Sheridan's eyes are on Anna. She is every part his wife, except the part that matters. The personality, the essence of the woman he loved, is gone, destroyed by being inside a Shadow ship. Sheridan reaches for the PPG hidden at his ankle as a door opens behind him. A Shadow creature edges into the room; Sheridan whips around, his PPG suddenly in his hand, and fires.

Ivanova asks G'Kar if the nuclear weapons can be used to destroy the Shadow vessels that surround Babylon 5. "That's what I've come to tell you," he replies. "Two of the devices are missing."

Sheridan, wounded and bleeding, staggers onto a parapet and looks out across the vast Shadow city beneath him. He toggles the controls on his link. Out in space, the White Star responds, and the nuclear weapons *on board arm themselves for detonation. "John," says a voice behind him. He turns to see Anna with her hand outstretched, walking toward him. "I know this isn't the Anna you knew. But I can love you as much as she did." Then a voice in his head—Kosh's voice—tells him to jump. Sheridan takes one last look at his wife and dives off the parapet, plummeting like a stone into the pit below. The* White Star *crashes through the dome above and explodes, encompassing everything within with the blinding power of two thermonuclear bombs.*

The Shadow vessels around Babylon 5 break off, shimmering back into hyperspace. Ivanova stares at the stars through the Observation Dome window. "He's gone," she says with tears in her eyes.

Sheridan is constantly warned about going to Z'ha'dum. First Kosh tells him, in Season Two's "In the Shadow of Z'ha'dum," that he would die if he went to the Shadows' homeworld. The warning is repeated in "Interludes and Examinations" and emphasized by Delenn's words to Sheridan in his flashforward in "War Without End." And yet he goes.

Joe Straczynski relates Sheridan's fateful decision to the classic story structure provided by the Greek myth in which Orpheus went into the underworld to retrieve his wife. "When any character appears before the oracle at Delphi and that character is told, 'Don't go into Hades,' you know they're going to go into Hades, because that's the structure of it. In this show, whenever you say to someone three times, 'Don't do this,' you know they're going to do it. It's like talking to a five-year-old: 'Don't put this bean up your nose, you'll turn blue and pass out.' When you come back, the kid's blue and on the floor! It just happens. So yeah, that you want to set up. He knows, and we know, that going to Z'ha'dum is going to be a really bad idea."

What he finds there is, perhaps, unexpected. This much-fabled planet, Z'ha'dum, where death awaits him, does not seem to be a version of Hades, or hell, at all. It is an almost homey place where a kindly old gentleman invites him to step inside and have some tea. His comment that tea helps him to sleep is a reflection of Sheridan's own statement about tea in "And the Rock Cried Out, 'No Hiding Place.'" They have brought him there not to kill him but to convince him that what they are doing is right. The wars, and the killing that results from them, may be horrific, but it can be argued that the Shadows have a point.

"Go back to Hegel, the philosopher, and his whole notion ties right into the Shadows," explains Joe Straczynski. "His whole expressed belief is that of conflict leading into the growth of the species. On the Net and elsewhere, there were people who said, 'Technically, yes, if you have a society in which there is no conflict, there really cannot be growth and evolution.' Technologically, all of our really significant advances came through warfare. The airplane was occasionally used here and there until World War I kicked it off. Atomic power was developed specifically through the need to have a weapon in World War II. War generates technology, technology generates cultural evolution, so you can make the argument that, on one level, they're right. They have, however, taken it to extremes, and that is the dividing line. So a lot of folks said, 'Technically, yeah, I see their point, *but* . . .'"

Justin, Morden, and Anna also present the argument regarding the Vorlons, spelling out what has largely been established throughout the season, that Humanity and other races have been manipulated by the Vorlons. They appeared as angelic beings and created telepaths among the other races because they needed them to fight *their* enemies. Morden describes the Vorlons as "control freaks," and there is something in that notion almost as repellant as the idea that war must be generated for its own sake.

"Neither side, the Vorlons or the Shadows, is actually correct," says Joe. "The notion that you must play by the rules and be nice, meaning play by *their* [the Vorlons'] rules, is wrong. And the idea you must have chaos and struggle, but do it according to the Shadows' rules, is also wrong. We have to make our own rules. It's in that dichotomy that the story of Babylon 5 takes place."

The device that lures Sheridan to Z'ha'dum is his wife. Anna Sheridan, as played by Beth Toussaint, had already been seen briefly in a recorded message in Sheridan's second episode, "Revelations." But for Anna's return from the dead, it was decided that Bruce Boxleitner's real-life wife, Melissa Gilbert, would be an interesting casting choice. There would be a certain preexisting connection between the two actors, and it would be good for publicity. "It was not anything I did," says Bruce. "This was strictly Doug Netter, Joe, and John Copeland's idea. At first, Melissa was going, 'What?' She was going, 'That's your territory, that's your place.' We've worked together before—it's not like we've never acted together before—but she felt kind of strange . . . But with some convincing from me and coaxing, Melissa said, 'Okay.' I thought it turned out fine, I really did. She delivered what she had to do, which was to deliver someone who wasn't really all there."

The fate of Anna Sheridan had always been in Captain Sheridan's back story. It was introduced in "Revelations" and resurrected fifteen episodes later in "In the Shadow of Z'ha'dum," when Sheridan discovered Morden had survived the destruction of her ship, the *Icarus*. These instances prepare for her return in a way subtle enough to make it believable, while retaining the dramatic impact of her walking through the door. Her arrival strikes up a new tension between Sheridan and Delenn, just at the point where they are making a commitment to each other. It brings welcome conflict into a relationship that, after the defining moment of the kiss, could have been in danger of losing its dramatic edge.

"Absolutely," says Mira Furlan. "I've said to Joe—and he agrees—that, from time to time, I have the feeling Delenn is going into this classical female role, really sweet, and that's not good. He's aware of that. Conflict is always good, and it should be. I don't want to lose her strength and the passionate side of Delenn and the energetic and strong and fierce side of Delenn to this gentle version of her. I love that, too, but if it's only that then it loses interest, and that's the danger. They can't always be these children, holding each other's hands and being happy."

The conflict is also within Sheridan. Faced with the return of the woman he loved and married, he does not know whether he should place his loyalties with Delenn or with Anna. Franklin's discovery in his medical examination of Anna soon resolves the problem for him, but the significance of Franklin's findings are not fully revealed to the audience until later in the episode. There is just a foreboding sense that something is wrong with Anna, something that is portrayed as much in the way Sheridan looks at her as it is in the dialogue.

Anna's emptiness is what keeps Sheridan distant from her, and this is where the Shadows fail. They do not understand that in destroying her personality, by putting her into one of their ships, they destroyed the very thing that could have made a connection with Sheridan. When Sheridan confronts them with this, they see that their ploy has failed. Sheridan fires at the Shadow creature in the room, and the next time the audience sees him, he is wounded, with his uniform torn and blood on his hands and face. This technique leaves the viewer to fill in the blanks.

"I wish we'd been able to see a shot of what had just happened," comments Bruce Boxleitner. "I thought, for myself, it was an abrupt cut. Me, as an audience, would have liked to have seen something other than just turning into the camera and firing the PPG. Maybe just a shot of that room in the aftermath. That was missing. And you know what? We literally had it planned, but we had some budgetary and time constraints and couldn't do it. That's one of those things where you think, 'Oh, I wish . . . !' "

When Sheridan stands on the parapet, there is, as Anna says, nowhere to run. Urged by the voice of Kosh in his mind, he makes the choice to jump to certain death, just as he did at the end of the second season. This is the hero sacrificing himself for others, an idea that runs strongly through the whole series. He knew exactly what he was doing when he left for Z'ha'dum. His farewell message to Delenn and his preparations regarding the nuclear weapons prove that. It just leaves the audience with one final question at the end of the season. Did he commit the ultimate self-sacrifice? Did he, as Kosh foresaw, die on Z'ha'dum?

ANNOUNCING THE PAST, PRESENT AND FUTURE OF...

BABYLON 5

ALL NEW EPISODES
BABYLON 5: THE FIFTH SEASON
WEDNESDAYS 10PM (ET)

THE SERIES: SEASONS 1-4
BABYLON 5
MONDAYS-SATURDAYS